PASSING THROUGH
PROVIDENCE

JOHN FULCO

Outskirts Press, Inc.
Denver, Colorado

This is a work of fiction. The events and characters described herein are imaginary and are not intended to refer to specific places or living persons. The opinions expressed in this manuscript are solely the opinions of the author and do not represent the opinions or thoughts of the publisher. The author has represented and warranted full ownership and/or legal right to publish all the materials in this book.

Passing Through Providence
All Rights Reserved.
Copyright © 2009 John Fulco
v2.0

Cover Photo © 2009 JupiterImages Corporation. All rights reserved - used with permission.

This book may not be reproduced, transmitted, or stored in whole or in part by any means, including graphic, electronic, or mechanical without the express written consent of the publisher except in the case of brief quotations embodied in critical articles and reviews.

Outskirts Press, Inc.
http://www.outskirtspress.com

ISBN: 978-1-4327-3629-3

Library of Congress Control Number: 2009928550

Outskirts Press and the "OP" logo are trademarks belonging to Outskirts Press, Inc.

PRINTED IN THE UNITED STATES OF AMERICA

1
Busing

The girls screamed, lifting their legs as the mouse scurried under their seats and down the floor of the school bus. The boys laughed and tried to stomp it. The driver opened the door, letting the critter escape into the morning light. "There he goes," Rossi said.

"Dumb mouse!" one of the girls shouted.

The students sat down and regained their composure. They were middle school kids, mostly minorities. It was their first week back after summer vacation.

Rossi Cataleno was in his second year as a school bus driver, and carrying a busload of kids was a big responsibility for anyone. He was fifty years old and finding employment was hard. He thought it was because of his age, but the bus company was willing to hire him if he did the training.

"My son is starting school today," Alicia, the monitor said. She came from the Dominican Republic when she was a little girl.

"How old is he?" Rossi asked.

"He's only four and in kindergarten."

"Well, that's good."

"My mother is happy, because she won't have to watch him every day."

"What's his name?"

"Andy," she said.

"Well, I hope he does well in school."

As he drove, the radio vibrated with the loud sounds of music. The kids always wanted to hear rap songs. Sometimes they sang too loud and he had to quiet them down. Most of the students on the bus came from different neighborhoods with different traditions; some came from distant countries like Columbia or Bolivia, speaking little English. They had to learn the language in school. Unfortunately, they learned some of the bad words first from their friends.

"Ross, do you like being a driver?" Alicia asked him for some reason.

"Do you really want to know?" he asked.

"Yes, tell me," she said, curiously.

"Well, I'm not crazy about it," he said. "When I was young, I never thought about driving a school bus. Who thinks about things like that?"

"Then why do it?" she asked.

"Because I'd rather work and pay my bills than go to the poorhouse. You know what I mean?"

"So here you are," she said.

"So here I am, the captain of my own ship. A big yellow boat with wheels on it and I'm hauling a load of kids to school."

She seemed surprised by his choice of words.

He looked far ahead for anything unusual in the road. Every day he wore a baseball cap to hide his baldness. Losing his hair, he thought, was like paying for a crime he didn't commit. Occasionally, he glanced into a large rearview mirror, seeing most of the kids seated behind him; each day was a different picture. He saw kids with happy faces, while others were sad; some had angry eyes and were mad at the world, but he saw some bright eyes in the group too.

"You know, we're just like babysitters," Rossi said. "We have to watch these kids for a few hours every day."

"I know," she said.

"And we have to write them up if they do anything wrong."

"You got that right," she said.

"We're not getting paid enough," he said.

"I know," she said.

"Sometimes I think I should have my head examined," he said.

Two boys in the road ran toward the bus and waved their arms. Rossi stopped and opened the door. As they came inside Alicia scolded them. "You know this is not where you catch the bus."

Rossi had a good memory and quickly recognized each kid. He studied their faces until he knew them. If he called them by their name, the better they responded.

"Good morning, Jason, glad to see you could make it."

"How'd you know my name?" the boy asked.

"I saw your bus pass the other day, remember?"

The boy sat down, looking confused.

Last year Rossi had trouble with a few of the boys fighting and had to suspend them from riding the bus. He hoped this year would be better.

When they arrived at the school, he turned off the radio and announced over the intercom, "Everyone remain seated." He held the microphone close to his mouth. "I just want to cover the rules with you." Standing up, he could see to the back of the bus. Some of the kids moaned with disapproval and shook their heads.

"Number one," he said, "you can't bring your mother with you on the bus." He looked serious, like a police officer giving a ticket. There was a moment of silence, then came some laughter from the girls.

"Number two, no smoking," he said.

Someone giggled.

"Number three, no smooching with the girls."

The boys looked at each other with smiles.

"Four, listen to this, because this really happened last year. Someone wanted to bring their dog with them. No pets allowed on this bus." One girl couldn't stop herself from giggling.

"No drugs on the bus either," he said. There was a moment of silence. "Now that I have your attention…" He pointed to a sign posted inside the bus. "The real rules are right there. Oh yeah, one more thing, no guns or knives. I don't want anyone going to jail. Okay, that's it. See you this afternoon."

The students were usually half asleep. Today, they were awake and talking as they left the bus. A tall girl smiled at Rossi on her way outside. The boys called her Easy Lucy. She had a good figure and was wearing a tight skirt.

"I think he looks like a movie star," said Lucy.

Alicia checked the empty seats for book bags. She found only candy and gum wrappers, which she threw into the trash can.

The early sun was getting brighter, so Rossi put on his sunglasses. He liked to fantasize, letting his mind drift off to some exotic land, where he sat on a beach drinking a beer, gazing at half-naked ladies laying in the sand.

"You ready to go?" his monitor said.

"What?" He jerked himself back to reality and started the bus rolling, going to his next school. He drove two routes in the morning and in the afternoon, taking the same students to middle and elementary school, then returning them home each day.

His second load of kids were smaller and sometimes more trouble than the bigger kids. The girls were okay—it was the boys who were always causing trouble. Some of them had no manners or teaching at home.

"Ah keee!" Carlos jumped from one seat to another. He was only six years old.

"Sit down and be quiet," Alicia said.

Carlos sat up with a smile on his face.

"You better stop playing around," she warned him.

Rossi was lucky he had a monitor who didn't sit there like a log. Sometimes, she had to yell at the kids to get them to listen. She even spoke to them in Spanish to make sure they understood.

Most of the time, the children were good on the bus. Charlie Simpson, the kid with the glass eye, was usually asleep with his good eye closed. Little Joanna had all her crayons on the seat and was coloring in her book.

"Ah keee!" Carlos kept jumping over seats.

"You get up here!" Alicia directed him. "You're sitting with me." The boy came forward, holding his head down. He just wanted to play.

"Some of these kids never listen," she said. "If there's any more trouble, I'll get the principal when we get to school." Now everyone acted like little angels.

Rossi turned the radio up, getting the kids' attention. The music helped to make the ride shorter by keeping them entertained.

When they arrived at the elementary school, Rossi opened the bus door, letting them go, then he checked the seats, making sure there was no one sleeping. Alicia went along with the smaller kids, walking them into school for breakfast.

When she returned, she asked him if he wanted to go somewhere for coffee. She was a single parent, struggling on state assistance, and he didn't want to spend more time with her, so he declined. Anyway, she was too young.

He drove a few blocks and stopped at an intersection. Something hit the windshield and cracked it. The headlight was hit and shattered into pieces, then he realized that someone was shooting at them.

He quickly reported what happened over the two-way radio. "Let's get the hell out of here!" he said, stepping on the gas.

2
Turner Yard

School buses pass through the streets of Providence every day, big yellow machines that rattle along and pick up children each morning. The buses even roll on weekends for field trips and sporting events. Most of them come from Turner Yard, a prosperous bus company that provides transportation for the capital city of Rhode Island. The yard is located next to some railroad tracks off Union Avenue in a low flat area with plenty of space. Trains pass by there every day on their way to New York.

A colossal gray structure stands in the center of the grounds surrounded by a sea of yellow buses that are parked in every direction like a maze. Most of the workers have to use the street and a dirt field to park their cars.

The building is divided into several parts, with employee lounges, offices, and a huge garage where the mechanics work on the buses. A pump station is near the rear of the building, where there's usually a line of buses waiting to be fueled.

There are short and long buses for use, flat-noses, and old GMC's. Most drivers like the newer flat-nose model, because it is easier to turn and drive.

Rossi was trained with a GMC that had the front hood and he liked using one. Every time he drove a flat nose, it broke down. He didn't know if the bus was that dependable or if he was a jinx.

"Mister Cataleno...."

He heard his name on the two-way radio in the bus.

"This is Ross," he answered.

"Where are you?" asked Kenny, the dispatcher.

"I'm parked in the yard," he said.

"The police caught the kid who was shooting at you with a pellet gun. See me when you come inside. I have a charter for you."

He only worked about thirty hours a week, so he didn't mind doing charters on nights and weekends for extra money. Sometimes he made forty hours or more.

Each charter was an adventure. Once he took a load of students from Brown University to see the Pawtucket Red Sox play. That was great, getting paid to watch the game.

He left his bus and walked toward the building. A couple of the drivers were washing their buses with a water hose behind the garage. He only washed his when it was necessary, like after it was hit with rotten eggs. Not that he was lazy, he just had better things to do. However, he made sure to sweep the bus and empty the trash can.

Jack Miller was walking on the roadway and waved at him.

"How you doing, Jack?" Rossi said.

"I had a bad run this morning," Jack said.

"What happened?"

"Some kid threw up on my bus, then I had to clean it."

"Lucky you, Jack."

"Damn kids, they're always getting sick on my bus. So, what's new with you?"

"The front of my bus was shot up this morning."

"No kidding. Everyone all right?"

"Yeah, but the bus needs a new windshield and headlight."

"Who did it?"

"The police caught some kid with a gun."

"Well, at least no one was hurt."

"So Jack, have you been to the track lately?" Rossi liked to play the horses.

"I was thinking of going tomorrow."

"What about next weekend?"

"That sounds good," Jack said, leaving. "We're betting the ponies next Saturday."

Rossi approached the building and entered the drivers' lounge. Bulletin boards and city maps covered most of the walls. A big screen television was in the corner and a green Ping-Pong table was on one side of the room. There were two wooden picnic tables on the floor and a refrigerator stood next to a counter with a coffeemaker.

It was Friday and payday. Everyone was smiling and saying hello. There were drivers who didn't know each other, but it didn't matter who you were, because you were respected by your peers.

A long line of people were waiting for their checks. Everyone was going into an office were the manager, Linda Stevens, was passing out white envelopes. She was a large friendly black lady, but today she wasn't too happy, because a few of the drivers had been caught recently with expired licenses.

"I want to see your CDL," she demanded, before paying each of them.

After receiving their checks everyone gathered around in ethnic groups, talking in their native languages. The Haitian drivers were parlaying French, and the Hispanics were speaking Spanish while playing a game of dominos on a picnic table, and three black men were using an African lingo that no one knew.

"Ross, here's your charter for tomorrow," Kenny said, handing him the paperwork. Kenny was a small black man with a short goatee, and he wore thick eyeglasses. He knew all the drivers and had the right temperament for the job.

"Thanks," Rossi said, looking at the sheet.

"If you have any questions, let me know," Kenny said.

Rossi folded the paper and put it in his pocket. He didn't stop to talk with anyone else. He was going to the bank to cash his check. It was only a couple of hundred, but it was enough to cover his household bills with some left over for groceries.

A few years ago he'd had a secure job at a city bank, but he was laid off with hundreds of other people. Unemployed for several months, he was desperate to find work, until one day he saw an ad in a newspaper for school bus drivers, then he was hired and became one. It wasn't easy, however; he had to study for hours to pass a long knowledge test, followed by a tough road test.

He cashed his check and headed home. He lived in Mount Pleasant, a better section of the city, where most of the houses were single-family homes with a few multi-families in between. Some of them were old, but well kept with cut lawns and trimmed hedges.

Rossi was glad he'd paid off his mortgage a few years ago, for he could never afford to live anywhere else. Some of his friends called him a cheapskate because he drove an old Ford Escort. The car ran good every year, so he forgot about buying a new one.

When he came to his place, he parked in the driveway. It was a two-family home and he rented the first floor to an elderly black lady with thin gray hair, who never had any complaints. He used her money for any repairs and to pay the taxes. Her hallway door was opened.

"Good morning, Ross," she greeted him from her kitchen. She loved company and always wanted to talk. She couldn't live without state assistance and a small Social Security check each month.

"How you feeling, Sadie?"

"I feel better than Superman," she said. "I've been flying high all night. Too much gin," she laughed. "Sit down and I'll make you some coffee."

"I can't this morning. I have things to do." He knew if he stayed, she would never let him go.

"Ah, you always have something to do. Nobody wants to talk anymore."

"Maybe next time," he said.

"You promise," she said, pointing a finger at him.

"I promise," he said, going upstairs.

His orange cat, Tommy Boy, ran toward him when he opened the door. The rooms were the same as downstairs, two bedrooms with a parlor, kitchen, dining room, and bath. It was ten in the morning and the cat was hungry. He fed him a plate of his favorite treat, then made himself a bowl of cereal. While eating, he watched the news on television. People were dying everywhere. Terrorist attacks in Israel, bombs dropping in some foreign city, and children starving to death. It was always the same news.

Sometimes he had bouts of loneliness and often thought of his ex-wife. She left him years ago, but he still missed her. She was just the opposite of him; she liked to dance and go places. He always wanted to stay home, watch television, and read books. He wondered if he would ever meet anyone else.

His toes started itching again. Inside his bedroom, he took off his socks, spraying some antifungal white powder on his feet, then changed into his sweat clothes. He liked to exercise and did some jumping jacks and a few push-ups. Starting to sweat, he went outside.

It was a beautiful day in the fall, good for jogging. As the squirrels were gathering their nuts and leaping through the trees, he ran down the sidewalk, taking long strides. He passed a row of homes and continued along the street, going by Mount Pleasant High School. Getting tired, he walked for a couple of minutes to regain his breath.

Cars were parked around the school and in the street. Morning classes were in session and he could hear voices. He wondered if any of the students were learning anything, for some of the kids on his bus seemed dumber than ever. He started to jog again, only slower this time, taking longer to get back home.

For awhile, he'd felt depressed, going without a job, but now he was doing better since he became a bus driver. He found time to fix things around the house and even planted some flowers in the yard. He played his harmonica and read more books.

Whenever he could afford it, he went shopping at a new grocery store in Olneyville that sold everything from soup to coconuts. He liked to go there for the fresh fruits and vegetables and usually filled his bags. Most ethnic brands could be found there too, canned and bottled goods from other countries. Hispanics loved the store and would load up their shopping carts and spend their whole week's pay there.

Sometimes his tenant, Sadie Smith, gave him a list of things she wanted, and he picked them up for her. "Make sure you stop and buy me a bottle of gin," she always reminded him.

He learned to cook in the army and was a pretty good chef. For lunch, he would fry eggplant and make sandwiches with tomato sauce and Parmesan cheese. Every day he had time to fix a meal for himself before returning to work.

The phone rang. He picked it up. "Hello," he said.

"Hello." It was a female voice.

"Who is this?"

"It's Lucy from the bus."

"How did you get my number?"

"From the phone book," she said. "Are you married?"

"No, and I don't think you should call here again," he said.

"Okay," she said. "See you on the bus. Bye."

He put the phone down. Strange girl, he thought.

3
Rock Attack

One afternoon Jack Miller was doing his run with a busload of children. He was a retired mailman and his pension was just enough to cover his regular bills. He was too young for Social Security, so he had to drive a bus. Besides, it was the only work available and he needed the money to support his gambling habit. He'd tried a job service company a few times, but it was only temporary.

He stopped his bus at an intersection and waited for a red light. He was watching the traffic when he heard a loud noise. He looked around and saw broken glass all over the seats. Someone was crying. When he pulled the emergency brake and opened the door, he saw two boys running away.

There was a broken window near the back of the bus.

"I want everyone to move up," he told the kids. "If you have to sit three in a seat, I want you to move up."

"She's bleeding!" a boy shouted.

A girl's face was bloody and she was crying. Jack rushed to open the first-aid kit. He found a large bandage and applied it to her head with pressure.

"You hold this bandage here," he told a boy, then moved to the front of the bus and called the dispatcher.

"Turner Yard, this is an emergency."

PASSING THROUGH PROVIDENCE

"What bus is this?" Kenny answered.

"This is fifty-eight. Some boys threw a rock and broke a window. A little girl got hit in the head. She's bleeding and I need a rescue truck ASAP!"

"What's your location?"

"I'm at Potters and Elmwood," Jack said.

"Hold on, I'm calling them now," Kenny said.

Jack started to sweat. He knew a school bus was an easy target, because it was big and slow. Any kid with a bad aim could hit one. He had a full head of gray hair and it was turning whiter by the day.

They had to wait for the rescue, and the children on the bus were getting restless.

"How long are we gonna be here?" a girl asked.

"We have to wait here, stupid," a boy said.

"I'm not stupid. You're stupid," she said.

Finally, the rescue truck came and two men climbed out. Jack told them what had happened. He gave the men the girl's name and address, then they transported her to the hospital.

He had to change buses, so he drove back to Turner Yard with the children and turned down the road to the building complex. It only took minutes and the dispatcher had another bus waiting for them.

"All right, everyone," Jack said. "Make sure you have your book bags. Don't leave anything."

The children stumbled forward from their seats, making the switch. Most of them had never been to the bus yard and couldn't wait to tell their teachers.

Jack was glad to get home that night. He wished he had saved his money—then he wouldn't have to work. He sat back in his easy chair and relaxed and drank a beer. It was quiet and he didn't have to listen to kids. He had a comfortable house in Johnston with a large living room, a fireplace, and two bedrooms.

His problems on the job were not as bad as his problems at home. For a long time he'd tried to stop smoking cigarettes. His doctor and wife wanted him to quit.

"Your father was a chain smoker and died from cancer," his wife Betty had warned him several times.

Eventually, he bought a pipe and tried puffing it, but it wasn't the same: cigarettes were better. When Betty was home, he'd smoked the pipe to make her happy. His other bad habit was gambling. He had lost thousands of dollars and was afraid to tell his wife. She knew he went to the horse track and the casino, but she didn't know how much he was losing.

"Oh, that smells nice," Betty said. "What kind of tobacco is that?"

"Cherry," he said.

"That really smells nice," she said again.

"Glad you like it," he said.

"I'm going to the store and pick up a few things," she said.

"You are? Then buy me some cigarettes."

"Yeah, right," she said, leaving.

He was reading a new book he'd received in the mail about gambling, studying it carefully, hoping to find a system to win. There had to be a way, he thought. He just had to find it.

4
Safety Meeting

The sound of railroad tracks echoed as the Boston train flew by the bus yard. A brown rabbit was frightened by the noise and ran across the ground, hiding behind some bushes.

Eva Gomez was walking to her bus when she saw Jack Miller. She was a tiny Puerto Rican woman with a pretty face and long black hair. She had flat breasts under her blouse and always wore tight-fitting blue jeans, showing a small waistline. It was still early in the morning, so she stopped to talk.

"What happened, Jack?" she said. "I heard you had trouble on your bus yesterday."

"Some boys were throwing stones and broke one of the windows. They hit a little girl."

"Was she hurt bad?"

"I think she'll need stitches."

"Where did it happen?"

"Elmwood and Potters," he said.

"Did anyone catch the boys?" she asked.

"No, not yet. They ran down the street."

"Well, I hope they catch them," she said, walking away.

Eva found her bus and started it, switching on the rear heaters. While she waited to get warm, she played the radio, listening to some Latino music.

Every day she thought about winning the lottery and buying a new house for her family. On Sundays she prayed in church for good luck. She even started a pool at work to buy tickets: she collected three dollars from each person for a chance to win millions. She was checking the numbers in the daily newspaper when the security guard walked up to her bus.

"Buenos Dias," he greeted her.

"Good morning, Pedro," she said.

"When are we gonna win?" he asked.

"Who knows?" she said.

"I hope it's soon."

"So do I," she said.

"I need a vacation," he said.

"Me too, Pedro."

"If we win, I'm going back to Columbia and retire," he said.

"Good luck, amigo." She had to leave and drove her bus around the building to pick up a monitor. They were shorthanded today and she had to go alone. It seemed like there were never enough monitors.

The little kids on her bus were loud that morning. She didn't know why. Maybe they had too much candy. They were always eating something.

"You have to be quiet," she told them several times.

The boys were playing and jumping in their seats.

"Sit down!" she hollered.

When they arrived at school, she was glad to see them go.

"Thank you, God," she said to herself.

When she returned her bus to the yard, management was holding their monthly safety meeting. The picnic tables were moved to one side in the lounge and rows of metal chairs were unfolded just for the occasion. There were coffee and donuts for the drivers. Eva took a jelly roll and sat down.

When all the chairs were occupied the manager, Linda Stevens, addressed them. Her voice was very deep and everyone could hear her. First she announced the names of the drivers who had worked for a year, awarding them with a certificate and a pin. She also gave awards for five and ten years. One man received a pin and a special gift for twenty years of service. Everyone applauded him.

The safety official was next. She talked about car drivers. "As you may have read in the newspapers," she said, "this state has thousands of uninsured cars on the road. Most of these drivers don't even have a license, so you have to be careful out there. No one cares if you're a good driver, but get into one school bus accident and you're on the national news, then the whole damn world knows about it!" She took a long breath, "And people with cell phones," she added, "you treat them the same as drunk drivers. Remember, the kids on the bus are our responsibility. We have to make sure they get to school safely. That's our job. By getting them to school, we get a good paycheck, right? Some of these kids will grow up and become part of the community. So you might say they're worth our time." She talked for another five minutes.

Afterwards, everyone had to watch a short film about school bus accidents.

"Okay, are there any questions?" Linda asked.

"Yes," a Hispanic man stood up. "I want to know who used my bus and left it full of trash?" He sounded angry and looked around at the crowd. No one answered him. "Next time, you better clean it up," he said.

"The boys are always fighting on my bus," a black lady said. "I can't do anything, they're bigger than me."

"Notify the principal when you get to school," Linda said. "You have to understand, if the kids are giving you trouble, the principal should suspend them from the bus."

The meeting ended after a few more questions and everyone was anxious to leave.

Eva drove home. When she was eighteen, she learned to drive and bought her own car. She rented a small cottage in Providence with her husband and children. She didn't mind being in the city, for it was closer to work.

She entered the house and found a pile of dirty clothes waiting for her. Before she did the laundry, she made some coffee for herself and drank a cup. She was getting addicted to caffeine.

While singing and picking up shirts, she noticed something. There was some lipstick on a sleeve. It must be lipstick, she thought, but whose? She never used much makeup, so it wasn't hers. She wondered if her husband was fooling around with another woman. He was still asleep in the bedroom, because he worked nights. She went in the room and threw the shirt in his face.

"Wake up, Luis," she yelled.

"What?" he said, opening his eyes.

"Whose lipstick is this on your shirt?"

"I donno," he mumbled, sitting up.

"It's not mine." She glared at him.

"Oh, I remember, I had a jelly sandwich at work and I messed my shirt," he said.

"You're a liar," she said.

"I'm not lying." He shrugged his shoulders.

"You'd better not be."

"I'm not," he said.

PASSING THROUGH PROVIDENCE

"Go to hell," she said, leaving the room. She was upset and didn't know what to believe. She went back to doing the laundry, but she wasn't singing anymore. She was raging mad with bad thoughts and felt he wasn't telling the truth.

5
Crazy Eyes

One September morning, Rossi was driving his bus through the streets, the big black wheels pounding the pavement. The traffic was loud and heavy; almost everyone was on their way to work.

He finished with the middle school and was doing his elementary kids. He was making frequent stops and picking up children every couple of blocks. The first kids on the bus were bored and fell asleep from the long ride. Only little Carlos was wide awake and talking to anyone who would listen. He was given Ritalin at home and sometimes his mother forgot to give it to him.

"Carlos, did you take your medication this morning?" Alicia asked him. She knew he hadn't. He just looked at her with a stupid grin on his face. She took him by the hand and sat him down next to her. "Be quiet," she told him.

Charlie Simpson, who had the glass eye, sat next to the window. He was a black kid and his good eye was alert, watching everyone. Some of the other kids were rude and called him Crazy Eyes.

Benjamin sat in the back seat. He was a fat white boy who weighed over two hundred pounds and was always sneaking food on the bus. Other kids called him the bomber and no one wanted to sit near him. Sometimes he was loaded with gas and farted so much that everyone had to open the windows.

PASSING THROUGH PROVIDENCE

"Benjamin, no eating," Alicia had to remind him every day.

"Anything you tell these kids goes in one ear and out the other," Rossi said.

"I know," Alicia said. "They don't care."

The gray sky disappeared and the sunlight was bright. Rossi slipped on his sunglasses. He was getting hot from the heat that was coming from the engine, so he slid open the side window for some air.

When he completed his run, the bus was full of sleepy children. He turned off Atwells Avenue and headed for the school.

"Wake up! C'mon, wake up!" Alicia shouted at them.

"School days, school days, dear old golden rule days," Rossi sang. The bus approached the playground at George West and moved along the curb.

"No standing!" Alicia yelled. "You wait until we stop."

"He's throwing papers on the floor," a girl said, pointing to a boy.

"Hector, if you don't pick up that mess, you're going to see the principal," Alicia said, warning him.

When no one was looking, Hector gave the girl the finger.

Rossi opened the door next to the sidewalk. Alicia stepped outside and the students slowly followed her.

Charlie Simpson was left behind. He was looking under the seats for something.

"What's the matter?" Rossi asked him.

"My eye fell out," the boy said.

"What the—? How'd that happen?" Rossi tried not to laugh.

"Can you help me find it?" The boy was on his knees searching the floor.

"It couldn't have rolled far," Rossi said, not trying to be funny.

"It popped out when I sneezed," the boy said.

"What's wrong?" Alicia saw them looking under the seats.

"His eye fell out," Rossi said.

"Oh my God!" Alicia said in disbelief.

Suddenly the boy stood up. "I found it," he said, holding the eyeball between his fingers.

"How can this happen?" Alicia asked. "I'm taking him to the nurse."

Rossi called the dispatcher. "I'm going to be late getting back to the yard," he said.

"Why, you have a problem?" Kenny asked.

"Yeah, a kid's eye fell out, so my monitor took him to see the nurse." He paused a second, then said, "By the way, it's a glass eye."

"Can you say that again?" Kenny said.

"I said a kid lost his glass eye on the bus. It fell out and rolled across the floor, but we found it."

"Now that's what I thought you said," Kenny said, laughing. "Take whatever time you need."

"Ten-four," Rossi said.

When Alicia returned, he drove the bus to a donut shop.

"That was funny," she said.

"I need a cup of coffee," he said.

"Me too," she said.

"I'm buying." He gave her the money. "And get a couple of donuts too."

He sat there and listened to the calls on the radio. He felt sorry for Charlie Simpson. The poor kid not only lost his eye, but his mother too in a car accident. His aunt was raising him now. Just then he heard a distress call on the two-way radio.

PASSING THROUGH PROVIDENCE

"Kenny, this is twenty-six, I had an accident. Do you hear me?" It was a woman's voice. There was no answer.

"Kenny, this is twenty-six," she said again.

"Go ahead," Kenny answered after a minute.

"I had an accident on Congress Street. It wasn't my fault. Some guy ran a stop sign and hit me."

"Ten-four, Congress Street," Kenny said. "Is anyone hurt?"

"Everyone's all right. No one is hurt," she answered.

"You wait there until the police come, okay?"

"Okay," she said. "I'm waiting here."

Alicia came back to the bus with donuts and coffee.

"The coffee smells good," Rossi said. He took a sip from his cup.

"I had to wait in a long line," she said.

"That's all right. We have time." He took a bite of his donut.

"By the way," she said. "I won't be in this afternoon. My mother is sick and I have to take her to the doctor."

"She's sick?"

"I think she has the flu."

"Then I'll see you tomorrow?"

"Yes," she said.

Driving back to Turner Yard, another school bus passed him. The driver pointed at Rossi. "I got my eye on you, nineteen." he said over the two-way radio.

"Hey Ross," someone else said. "Like they say in the navy, eye, eye sir."

"Very funny, guys," Rossi answered them, driving into the yard.

"That's space bus nineteen," someone else said.

"You got that right, man."

"All right, knock it off," Kenny said, laughing. "Stay off the air."

After dropping Alicia at the monitors' lounge, Rossi found a place to park. He carried an old broom on board to sweep the floor. Besides some trash every day, he found coins which he used to buy books at a flea market. Once he found a used condom and another time a bloody tampon. Nothing surprised him anymore. He left the bus carrying a plastic bag full of trash.

After a few steps, he came across Kenny and another driver.

"Ross, we're short buses, so I need to use yours for a charter," Kenny said.

"I just cleaned it," he said.

"Don't worry," Kenny said. "We'll make sure it's clean and back on time for your afternoon run."

"I hope so," Rossi said, on his way to the dumpster. He threw the bag into it, before going to the drivers' lounge. Every day he saw the same mix of people inside the building.

The Haitians were sitting and watching television, while the Puerto Ricans were playing cards at a table. Some drivers were reading newspapers, and a guy was filling the coffeepot with water. They were waiting around, hoping to get extra work.

Lenny Harris, the driver trainer, had several new faces seated at a table. Each morning he took them for driving lessons on the bus. He was checking their permits and giving them instructions. They were paid minimum wage while training.

"Hey Ross," Lenny motioned to him. "Come over here a minute."

"What's up?" Rossi said.

"I heard some kid lost his eyeball on your bus," Lenny said, and everyone in the room started laughing.

"Oh, here we go again," Rossi said, walking away.

He headed for the time card clock, located next to the dispatcher's office. When he found his card, he ran it through the slot. He just wanted to get away from there.

Getting into his Escort, he went home. The car was running good, but it was burning a quart of oil every month. His tenant, Sadie Smith, met him at the door and offered to make him breakfast. She never had much company and most of her friends were dead. "Now there's no one left to bring flowers to my funeral when I die," she often said.

"So, how are you feeling today, Sadie?" he asked.

"Well," she said, "my neck hurts and my back hurts, other than that, I feel just fine for an old lady."

"Well, I hope you live to be a hundred," he said.

"Well, hell yeah, as long as I have enough gin, I might do that," she said in good humor. "So how's those kids on the bus doing?"

"You don't want to know." He smiled.

"That bad, huh?"

"Worse," he said.

She was always sweeping or mopping. She lived there for several years and kept her apartment clean. Rossi sat down at the kitchen table.

"How would you like your eggs?" she asked him.

"Over easy," he said.

She lit a burner and put a frying pan on it.

"So Ross, when you getting married again?"

"Married?" he said, surprised. "Why I don't even have a girlfriend."

"You know you're a good-looking guy," she said. "If I was younger, I'd marry you myself."

She finished cooking and put the plate in front of him. He ate and she talked, especially about her childhood and her old boyfriends.

"Your cooking is real good," he said, finishing the last slice of toast.

"My kitchen is always open," she said.

"I don't need reservations?" he said, leaving.

"No reservations." She laughed.

He went upstairs to his apartment and opened a window to change the air. There were some dirty pots and pans in the kitchen sink. Tommy Boy, his orange cat, was sitting on a chair.

"Hello, fella." He patted him on the head. The cat stood and stretched. "You want something to eat?"

"Meowww." The cat's ears perked up.

He opened a can of fish and fed him. "How's that, good?" he said. "Now where did I put my harmonica?"

He went searching through the house until he found it. He'd bought the instrument a year ago and was getting better at playing it. He put it to his mouth and blew a sad melody.

There was a ringing noise. It was the phone. He picked it up and the line was silent. Deep down inside, he was hoping it was his ex-wife.

6
The Casino

A boy on Jack Miller's bus was being bullied by two other boys.

"What's the matter? Can't talk?" they teased him.

The boy tried to move away to another seat. They grabbed him and pummeled him with several blows. The boy pushed back, trying to get free. The other kids were yelling, "fight-fight-fight!"

Jack didn't have a monitor. He stopped the bus and moved quickly.

"Everyone sit down, I'm coming through," he said. "That's enough, you two. Up front, now!" he raised his voice. The two boys glared at him and didn't move. "Do you want me to get the police?" Jack said. Reluctantly, the boys went to the front and sat down.

After a few weeks of school, Jack thought about quitting. He was fed up with some of the boys on the bus. He felt like he was a father again, raising his kids. He didn't need the aggravation. He had enough headaches with all the money he was losing.

The casino Jack went to was in Connecticut and called Stony Brook. It was run by a small tribe of unknown Indians and backed by big-time investors. It sprang up overnight like a giant, gaudy-colored circus tent. The attraction was unbelievable and people came by the thousands. Long lines of cars came there like rats to cheese with methodical people who were programmed to follow orders—"Bring your hard-earned cash and leave it here. Your life savings too!"

That's what Jack did. He lost his money in the slot machines, then tried the table games. He played blackjack almost every night and on weekends. He tried one system after another. Sometimes he won, but he lost more often.

He even tried the dice table once and caught a hot roll. Everyone was winning. They were excited and yelling numbers as the dice rolled across the table. Jack couldn't believe how much he had won. When he left the casino, he was nine hundred dollars richer.

One day he came home with a roulette wheel. It was just like the one in the casinos, only smaller. The game intrigued him with so many numbers.

"What are you going to do with that, Jack?" Betty asked.

"Practice," he said.

"You have got to be kidding," she said, laughing.

"It works the same way as a real one," he said.

"You're always going to the casino. I hope you're winning."

"Sometimes," he said.

"If you start losing, you better quit."

"Of course I will," he lied.

"You should spend more time at home. I'm always here by myself," she complained.

"I know," he said, going into another room.

He set the roulette wheel on a table and spread out the green cloth with the numbers on it. There must be a way, he thought to himself as he studied the numbers. It was like cracking a safe. He just had to find the right combination to get the money.

PASSING THROUGH PROVIDENCE

After a few hours of spinning the tiny ball around on the wheel, he thought he had it. He went back to the casino like a soldier going to battle, armed with knowledge and a winning system. He started playing with a set amount of chips. Before long, he was defeated, losing again. Playing with real money was completely different.

He went home brooding and spent several days lying around the house with his head full of doubt. A few weeks later, he saved some money and regained his confidence. He went back to the casino feeling good about himself, but he didn't win.

His drinking, smoking, and gambling habits were starting to give him a case of the nerves. He had an endless supply of credit cards and was going deeper in debt, making cash advances from some cards to pay others. He was sleeping less, maybe five hours a night, and was having bad dreams about his old job delivering mail. Dogs were chasing him down the street, biting his legs. He woke up one night in a cold sweat.

"What's the matter, honey?" Betty asked him.

"I'm having nightmares," he told her. "I'm carrying the mail again. And it gets worse, I'm attacked by mad dogs."

His wife tried to comfort him. She gave him some Tylenol with water, then rubbed his back for awhile.

"I hope you sleep better," she said.

7
The Company Trainer

Lenny Harris was the official company trainer. After doing his run in the morning, he was paid extra to teach new drivers. The group waited in the lounge, sitting around a picnic table. When they finished with their coffee, Lenny checked their permits, then they loaded onto a bus. He drove them across town to Pleasant View School where an empty parking lot was located. The class was always small, several people or less. This time, there were four Hispanic and two white men and a black woman.

After stopping the bus, Lenny stood before them, a bald-headed black man of average height. "You have sixty days until your permits expire," he said. "With my expert help, you should all be bus drivers in half that time. Any questions?"

"When do we have to pass a road test?" a man asked.

"When I think you're ready," Lenny said.

"What if I don't pass?"

"If you don't pass, you can take the test a week later," Lenny said to assure them. "Now for today, I want you to get familiar with the bus. Each one of you will get a turn behind the wheel. "You go first," he told the woman.

"Me," she said, surprised.

"Yes, you," Lenny said. "Just follow my instructions and show these guys how to do it."

"Okay," she said, sitting in the driver's seat. She seemed afraid but was willing to try.

"The first thing you do is put on your seat belt, then turn on the key," Lenny said. "Now I want you to drive slowly forward."

She put the bus in gear, pushing her foot down on the accelerator.

"That's good. Not too fast. Turn onto that side road." Lenny directed her with his finger. "Go down that way and come back into the parking lot."

She drove around onto a short dirt road that ran next to a golf course. It felt like riding a big boat to her. A short time later, she came back into the parking lot.

"Keep going, girl. One more time around. I want you to get used to it. Don't worry guys, you'll get your turn." Lenny chuckled.

After everyone drove through the loop several times, Lenny turned off the engine. "Let's move outside," he said, going to the front of the bus. The group followed him.

"What are we doing now?" the lady asked.

"We're doing this," Lenny said, opening the hood. "The pre-trip," he said. "This is the first part of your test for your license. You have to name the parts of the engine, like air filter, water pump, oil stick. You have to know where they are or you won't pass."

"You mean, to drive a bus, I have to know about the motor," the lady moaned.

"That's right," Lenny said. "It's not hard. It just takes a few weeks of practice, by then you should know everything."

"You really have to do this?" a man asked.

"What did I just say?" Lenny said. "To get your CDL, you have to know it. Just point your finger at the part and name it. You'll learn sooner than you think."

"Oh man," the lady said, shaking her head. "I don't believe this."

"It's a piece of cake," Lenny said. "If I can do it, you can do it." He walked around the bus with the group following him. He showed them how to identify all the lights and mirrors. "You have to check the wheels too, the lug nuts and tire tread. You'll learn more every day. Okay, now I'll point to something and you tell me what it is."

"How much time do we have for this test?" the lady asked.

"Ten minutes," Lenny said.

The group looked at him in disbelief.

"Only ten minutes," the lady said.

"You can do it," Lenny said. "We practice every day. Nothing to it. You know, in the past five years, I've helped over a hundred drivers get their license."

After going around the bus for an hour and identifying parts, the group went inside.

"Now, this is your dashboard," Lenny said. "It has all the toys. You have to get familiar with them and learn what the gauges and buttons are for."

That night Lenny drove home in his red Cadillac. He was raised in an orphanage and had no family. When he was a teenager he needed money, so he dealt drugs and tried to make his way in the world, until someone tried to shoot him.

He escaped death and tried several different jobs. Once he was employed by the state as a prison guard. The job paid well, but it was dangerous. Guards were always getting attacked by inmates, so he quit and became a bus driver.

PASSING THROUGH PROVIDENCE

He lived over in Clown Town. The houses were painted wild colors, like lime green, purple, or bright orange. It was the seamy part of town where prostitutes worked the streets at night and drugs were sold. He parked his Caddy in front of his house. The car was his pride and joy and was only a few years old. It looked new, but it had over a hundred thousand miles on the engine and was costing him big bucks for repairs.

He went upstairs to his flat on the second floor, where he shared two bedrooms with a buddy. It was just a place to sleep with little furniture and nothing to eat in the refrigerator.

He took a quick shower, changing into clean clothes and slapping on some cologne. He had several girlfriends and was thinking about going to Carmella's house. There was a knock in the hallway.

"Who's that?" He moved toward the door.

"Is Rudy Smith there?"

He heard a man's voice. "He's not home," Lenny said.

"It's the police. Can we talk with you?"

He opened the door, facing two men in uniform.

"Do you know where Rudy is?" they asked him.

"I wish I did, he owes me money."

"Can we search your apartment?"

"Sure, but he's not here."

"When did you see him last?" they asked him while they looked through the rooms.

"It's been a couple of days," Lenny said.

When the officers didn't find anything, they left and went down the stairs.

Lenny wondered why they were looking for Rudy. He knew that his buddy wasn't dealing drugs. He looked out the window and saw their car pull away.

His girlfriend lived close to the bus yard. He left his place and drove to a barbecue joint, where he bought a roasted chicken with potato salad.

He parked his red Caddy in front of her apartment house and took the bag of food with him to the second floor, then knocked on the door.

"Who's there?" she asked

"Carmella, it's me," he said.

"Yes, who's me?"

"It's Lenny."

8
A Desperate Man

Eva drove her bus to the Y.M.C.A. She was a short person, so a thick wooden block was wired to the gas pedal for her foot to reach. She parked in front of the building where she waited for a load of daycare kids. She was going to take them home to their parents.

Five years ago, she came to this country with her family. She was grateful for the money she earned driving a bus; it was better than working in a factory. She made enough to pay for a car and get new clothes for her kids. She even had more time to spend with her family.

She was waiting in her seat and thinking about Luis. Was he cheating on her? She wondered.... A man knocked on the door. She opened it and he came up the stairs pointing a gun at her.

"Let's go! Drive the bus!" he ordered her.

She sat there in shock and couldn't move.

"I said, let's go!" He seemed desperate and waved the gun around with his hand.

"Go where?" she said in disbelief.

"Take me to the hospital," he ordered her.

"The hospital," she heard herself mumble. Her hands were shaking now. This guy must be loco, she thought.

"Let's go!" he said again, getting angry.

"But I'm waiting for some kids here," she said.

"You see this," he said, putting the gun in her face. "It's not a toy!"

"Okay, okay, I'm going. You can put it down," she said, starting the bus. Her heart was pounding as she pulled into the street.

"Get on ninety-five," he said, standing behind her.

"Okay," she said again. I-95 was right around the corner from the Y.M.C.A.

"Hurry up, bitch!" he shouted at her.

When they were on the freeway, she wondered why he wanted to go to the hospital. The man had a long scar on the side of his face. He didn't look like he was injured or anything.

"Come on, faster," he said, pushing the gun barrel into her back.

"Okay, I'm going faster," she cried, the tears coming down her face. Was he going to shoot her? She thought about stopping the bus in the middle of the busy freeway, but it might cause an accident. It was only a short distance to the exit.

"Turn off here!" He waved his gun.

She drove down a ramp onto a side street, then around to the hospital's main entrance.

"Stop! Let me out!" he ordered her.

She pulled up and opened the door. He left, running into the main building.

She was shaking and sobbing. It only took minutes, but it seemed a lot longer. Quickly, she pulled herself together, drying her eyes with a tissue. She called the dispatcher over the two-way radio.

"This is an emergency," she said.

"What's the problem?" asked Kenny.

"This is Eva," she said. "Some guy jumped on my bus at the Y.M.C.A. He had a gun and made me drive him to the hospital."

"Eva, you're saying some guy hijacked your bus at gunpoint?"

"That's right," she said. "He had a gun."

"Eva, where is he now?" Kenny asked.

"He jumped out and ran into the building."

"Okay, stand by, Eva, I'm calling the police. Don't move until they come. All right?" Kenny said, concerned.

"Okay, I'm staying here," she answered. She waited and tried to remain calm.

The police came fast, first one car, then another. She told them the man had a gun and made her drive here. Two of the policemen hurried into the building.

"This sounds like the guy we're looking for," one of the officers said. "He robbed a drugstore a couple of blocks from the Y.M.C.A." They wrote down her name and address and any information she could give them. After some questions, the police thanked her for her help.

She drove back to the bus yard and was feeling too upset to work, so she went home.

9
Betting Buddies

After jogging Saturday morning, Rossi took a shower and shaved before dressing, then picked up Jack Miller. They were going to play the horses.

"You feeling lucky today?" Jack said.

"I hope we do better than last time," Rossi said.

"Ross, didn't we break even last time?"

"Yeah."

"Well, that's not losing," Jack said.

"It's not winning either," Rossi said.

They stopped at Samford's in Cranston for breakfast. The restaurant was always busy on weekends. They had low prices and good food. The dining room was packed with hungry faces, and smells of bacon, toast, and coffee filled the air. The hostess led them to a table.

"What a goldmine," Jack said, sitting down.

"You know it," Rossi said.

The waitress came at once and took their orders, then brought them some coffee. Rossi added cream and sugar to his cup. He had a good appetite and was usually hungry after jogging.

Jack had the racetrack paper with him and studied the charts at Suffolk Downs. His face was buried between the pages as he concentrated on the latest workouts.

"Do you see anything good, Jack?"

"There's a couple of races I like, but I can't be sure until I see the track odds."

"We need winners this time," Rossi said.

"Well, the program looks good." Jack was full of confidence.

The waitress came with two platters of food.

"Here you go, fellas," she said, putting the dishes down in front of them. "Enjoy," she said, smiling.

"Looks good," Rossi said, digging into his eggs.

They both had a large omelet with home fries and toast. Jack put ketchup and extra pepper on his eggs. Rossi smeared strawberry jam on his toast. They both ate fast and cleaned their plates. They finished their coffee while waiting for the bill. After leaving a tip for the waitress, they were on their way.

Rossi drove north on I-95 out of Rhode Island. As the car went along, Jack was talking about busing. "You know, it's nothing but a big scam," he said. "Ninety percent of those kids can walk to their local schools."

"You know that, Jack, and I know it, but we need to work, so don't tell anyone else."

One hour later, they were going through Boston and the traffic was bad. Rossi's car was in the only lane that was moving, and he managed to get there on time. They walked through the rows of cars and headed for the grandstand.

It was a good day for racing. People came there from everywhere and from all walks of life to play the horses. It was the sport of kings and anyone who wanted to bet two bucks. People milled together, talking and studying their papers. Hitting a big daily double—the winner of the first and second races—was everyone's dream. Once inside, Jack found his way to the bar.

"I'm buying," he said, paying for the beer. He lit a cigarette and looked at the tote board. "I think the favorites are gonna take the double today."

"I hope you're right, Jack."

"Let's drink up and get out tickets."

"Here's to good luck," Rossi said.

They both drained their glasses, then went to get in line. Rossi counted his money again; he wanted to save some for gas. They played five bucks each on the double and made their way outside.

"The horses for the first race are in line," the announcer said. The favorite jumped out to the front and led all around the track to the finish line.

"We won," Rossi said.

"Let's have another beer." Jack headed for the bar.

"I hope we hit the double."

"It won't pay much if we do, because they're favorites," Jack said.

"Well, winning is better than losing," Rossi said.

People were crowded around inside, watching a replay of the race on a giant TV screen. Some of them were happy because they'd won, but most of them had long faces.

The second race was a photo finish. Everyone waited for the final results.

"We won by a head," Jack said. "The double paid twenty-one, forty." He did some adding with his pencil. "Not bad, we each made over fifty bucks."

"I can take that," Rossi said with a smile. He bought a cigar at the bar and lit it.

"I can't believe you're smoking that stogie," Jack said.

"Why not, I feel like a winner," Rossi said, puffing his cigar.

"So, who do you like in the next race?"

"The horse I like is second choice. He might pay a good price, so I'm betting him."

"I hope you're right, Jack, because I'm putting five bucks on him."

They bought their tickets and went outside again with the crowd. It was a short race, five furlongs. The horses left the starting gate and galloped around the track. In no time, they were coming down to the wire. There was an uproar from the crowd and then silence as everyone held their breath.

"It was close, but we won again," Rossi said, smiling.

"That horse was supposed to win," Jack said, full of confidence. "He had the best workout time. C'mon, let's cash our tickets."

After getting their money, they returned to the bar for another drink. Rossi just sipped his beer because he had to drive home. His buddy checked the paper for more clues.

"Ross, it looks like I got one in this race too."

"Which one?"

Jack was talking with a cigarette dangling from his mouth. "You see this horse here." He pointed his finger in the paper.

"The six horse," Rossi said.

"Yeah, the six. He has the best time for the race, but he never ran at this track before, and he's gonna be a long shot."

"You betting him, Jack?"

"I'm thinking about it."

"Well. I have to go pee," Rossi said.

Jack looked at the digital clock on the wall. "You have five minutes before the race," he said.

"I'll meet you back here," Rossi said, leaving. A sea of noisy bodies moved across the floor. He mixed into the flow and disappeared.

The restroom was packed with impatient men, and the stench of urine filled the air. Some of them waited in line to relieve themselves. Rossi took his turn and left.

An old crazy guy was speaking to everyone near him. "Losers, you're all losers," he kept saying. He was either drunk or senile, and the crowd tried to avoid him.

Rossi found his way back to the bar. His buddy wasn't there, so he went outside to see the post parade. The horses were walking slowly with their jockeys on them, passing the grandstand and heading toward the starting gate. The six horse stopped momentarily, lifted his tail, and unloaded a pile of dung on the ground.

Rossi had heard this was a good sign. The six had the best time, Jack told him. He dropped his cigar and ran inside to the ticket counter. He glanced up at the odds board. The favorite was even money, but the six was completely overlooked and was thirty to one. He had less than a minute before the race and bought the tickets just in time. He bet five bucks to win and played the exacta.

The floor was empty now—everyone was watching the race. He rushed through a door to the track and a wall of noise hit him as the race started. His heart dropped when he saw the six running last. The horses ran around the first turn leaving a cloud of dust. Halfway through the six was still last, but then he started to move up on the outside. They galloped around the far turn and his horse was at the head of the pack. Coming into the stretch, they were all bunched up. He wasn't sure who was leading and held his breath as the horses came down to the finish line. It was a close race and he couldn't believe his eyes: the six won by a neck.

He looked through the crowd hoping to see his buddy. He wanted to tell him about his good luck. When the official results were posted, he felt fantastic. His horse paid sixty-five dollars to win. He quickly did the math. His five dollar ticket was worth over a hundred and sixty bucks and the exacta paid almost six hundred. He couldn't believe it and wanted to celebrate. He went back to the bar and found Jack there, drinking a beer.

"Did you bet the six?" Rossi asked him.

"I wish I did," Jack said, turning his thumbs down. "I lost ten bucks on the favorite."

"Well, I bet him," Rossi said, "and I won big time." He showed his buddy the tickets.

"I didn't bet him," Jack said, "because he was thirty to one. I thought something had to be wrong."

"I hit the exacta too."

"You did?" Jack said in disbelief. "I think it paid over five hundred bucks."

"Five hundred and eighty-five dollars, to be exact."

"How the hell did you pick that second horse?"

"Just a lucky guess. I played the three because I liked his name."

"His name…" Jack looked at the program. "Busboy," he said.

"You get it," Rossi said. "I'm a bus driver and I saw Busboy."

"I get it, you lucky ass. You're buying us a round."

"You got that right, the beers on me."

Rossi bought another cigar and was puffing on it when he cashed his tickets. It felt good to be a winner. He folded the bills into his front pocket and went back to the bar.

"I'm hungry. How about a couple of hot dogs?"

"Sounds good to me," Jack said, swallowing his brew. "And another beer."

Rossi ate his dog with the works and enjoyed every mouthful.

"They always taste better at the track," Jack said, sprinkling celery salt over his dog.

"I'm getting one more," Rossi said.

"That's enough for me." Jack guzzled his next drink down like water and was getting loaded.

Rossi didn't want to blow all the money he won, so he didn't bet anymore. He was content with just smoking his cigar and watching everyone.

His buddy played a few more races and ended up losing. "That's it," he said, drinking his beer. "I'm not betting another dime. I'm ready to go home, but I have to pee first." Feeling lightheaded, Jack walked through the crowd and almost lost his balance.

"You all right?" Rossi asked, trailing him.

Jack didn't say anything. He staggered into the men's room and rushed to a toilet bowl, fell to his knees, and threw up.

Rossi decided to wait outside the door, smoking his cigar. His buddy took awhile. Finally, he appeared confused and with his face red as a beet.

"What's the matter?" Rossi asked him.

"I think I lost my plate. Hell!" he said, going back into the restroom.

"You lost what?" Rossi followed him.

Jack went to the toilet bowl, bent over, and plunged his hand into the murky pool and fished around, pulling out his false teeth. He turned on the hot water in the sink and washed them for a few minutes. When the plate cooled down, he popped it back into his mouth. Rossi busted out with laughter.

"What's so funny? That plate cost me a couple of hundred," Jack said.

Rossi kept laughing, he couldn't control himself. For most of the way home, he was smiling, thinking about his buddy.

10
An Old Girlfriend

As Rossi walked through the rows of buses, a tall black girl approached him. He didn't know her name, but he knew she was a new driver.

"I can't find my bus," she said.

He smiled at her. "Let me help you out," he said. "It has to be around here. I think it looks like a big yellow block of cheese with round black wheels."

"Very funny," she said, giggling.

"I drive bus nineteen," he said.

"Have you been doing it long?" she asked.

"This is my second year."

"Is it a tough job?"

"Sometimes it can be, every day is different."

"How are the kids?"

"There's good and bad kids, sometimes it's like a zoo on the bus," he said.

"A zoo, what do you mean?"

"You know, the kids, they get out of control."

"Oh, I see," she said. "Now I'm not so sure about this job."

"I'm not trying to discourage you. I'm just telling you what to expect."

"Well, thanks anyway." She seemed disappointed and walked away.

Rossi found his bus in the back row. It wasn't where he had left it. He checked the sides for any damage, because someone took his bus once and put a dent in it. Everything looked okay, but the fire extinguisher was missing. There was a lack of security at Turner Yard and sometimes, there was a lot of theft and vandalism.

Before starting the bus, he removed his coat. It was ten degrees warmer inside with the sun. He checked the brakes, turn signals, stop arm, and fuel gauge. If someone used his bus, he had to be extra careful.

When he was satisfied with everything, he drove behind the building where there was a line of buses waiting to get a monitor. As they were waiting, a loud train whirled by the yard. He could see dark figures in the square windows of the cars, like passing silhouettes in the afternoon light.

A group of ladies were smoking and standing outside the building. Rossi pulled up and didn't see Alicia. The manager came forward and assigned someone else to go with him. One of the ladies put out her cigarette and stepped into his bus. She looked familiar.

"Hello," she said, taking a seat.

"I think I know you," he said. "Well, I'll be damn, Laurie."

"Ross, I don't believe it!"

"What a small world," he said. She was an old girlfriend.

"You look younger," she said.

"I lost a few pounds, because I've been working out."

"Ross, I thought you had a banker's job."

"They let me go. Hundreds of us, downsized," he said.

"That's too bad, after all those years you worked there."

"Yeah, tell me about it," he said.

"So why didn't you get a job at another bank?"

PASSING THROUGH PROVIDENCE

"I tried, but they wouldn't hire me. I was out of work for months and now, I'm a bus driver."

"Do you like doing this?"

"I like the shorter hours, but sometimes I have to deal with dumb kids," he said.

"Bus nineteen," the dispatcher called him.

"Yes, go ahead," he replied.

"You have a new stop tomorrow. See me when you get back."

"Ten-four," Rossi answered. "So, Laurie, whatever happened to you? You just disappeared on me."

"I got married, but now we're separated," she said.

"Well, that didn't last long," he said.

"No, it didn't."

"So what happened?"

"He's in jail for drugs."

"He was selling drugs?"

"Yes, I should have never married him."

He could see the worried look on her face. "You should have married me," he said, trying to cheer her up.

"I made a mistake," she said.

"Do you ever go to see him?"

"One time I did, but his mother was there and she thinks it's my fault he's in jail."

"So you don't plan on getting back together again?"

"No way," she said. "He's too much trouble."

There was another call on the two-way radio for someone. She gazed out the window for a few minutes.

"Cheer up," he said. "Better days are ahead."

"I hope so," she said.

She was in her late thirties and slender. She had a light complexion and long black hair with a plain face. Her mother was Irish American and her father Mexican. She must have taken after her mother, for she had deep blue eyes.

"You know, I'm glad we met again," Rossi said. "Maybe we can go out sometime."

She didn't say anything.

"Fifty-three to dispatcher," a voice came over the two-way. "Because of traffic, I'm going to be ten minutes late for my school."

"Ten-four," Kenny answered.

He drove to his middle school where other buses waited along the street. He parked behind them just as the students came out from the building. The kids ran across the grounds toward the buses, playing and shouting names.

"How you doing?" Easy Lucy greeted Rossi.

"Take a seat," he told her.

The first group of kids on always headed for the rear seats; they fooled around the most. In a short time, the buses were full. The drivers had to wait for the principal's signal to leave, but there was a problem. No one was moving.

The radio was loud. Suddenly, Rossi pulled out his harmonica and blew into it, keeping time with the music, winking his eye at Laurie. Everyone seemed surprised. The students started clapping their hands. Easy Lucy and another girl were dancing in the aisle. A boy grabbed the broom, pretending to play it like a guitar. Everyone was having a good time, until someone banged on the door. Rossi turned the radio down and opened the door. It was the principal.

"What's going on here?" he asked.

"We were just leaving," Rossi said, driving away.

"I didn't know you played the harmonica," Laurie said.

"Well, I've been practicing," he said.

"I guess so," she said.

"He plays pretty good," a girl said, overhearing their conversation.

He stopped the bus to drop off the Thomas brothers, but they weren't there. "What happened to the twins?"

"They're on detention and have to stay after school," someone said.

"Those boys are always in trouble," Rossi said.

"Can you put the music back on, please?" someone asked.

He turned on the radio.

There was a black boy who sat alone. He was big and mysterious and never talked with anyone. He wore a hooded sweatshirt that covered his face and you could never really see him.

"What's his name? The kid with the hood," Rossi asked the girl behind him.

"Oh, that's JoVon," she said. "He doesn't say much."

Easy Lucy was sitting in the lap of a boy.

"What's she doing?" Laurie stood up and made her way toward the back. The girl's body was moving up and down on the boy's lap. "What do you think you're doing?" Laurie asked.

"I'm giving him a lap dance," Lucy said. "I want to see how big his thing is."

"You come up front and sit with me," Laurie said.

"Okay," Lucy said.

Rossi just shook his head.

"Now I've seen everything," Laurie said.

They came to the next school at three o'clock with the bus empty again. A teacher marched toward them with a line of children following her.

"Are these your kids?" she asked Rossi.

"No, I never saw them before," he said laughing, "but I'll take them."

"Lucky you," the teacher said, glad to be rid of them.

"Lucky us," Laurie said as the children came on the bus, pushing and teasing each other. Someone was howling like a dog. Another kid was making sounds like a rooster. Big Ben was eating a bag of chips.

"This is my elementary run," Rossi told Laurie. "Some of these kids are so funny, they're hysterical."

"All right, let's quiet down!" Laurie shouted. "You put those chips away," she told Ben. "No eating on the bus!"

"Who's barking like a dog?" Rossi said.

"Crazy Eyes is doing it," Carlos said.

"Stop that noise, Charlie Simpson," Rossi said.

"Where's Alicia?" Ben wanted to know. "She couldn't make it today," Laurie said.

"I have to pee…" a small voice was heard.

"Who said that?" Laurie asked. A little hand came up. It was Joanna, a first grader.

"You have to go to the bathroom?"

The child nodded her head.

"C'mon, follow me." Laurie took her hand and led her back to the school.

After a few minutes, the kids were growing restless, so Rossi turned on the music and started playing his harmonica. The smaller children seemed fascinated when they heard him play and grew quiet. He was like the Pied Piper and they came under his spell.

When he stopped to catch his breath, Carlos asked, "What is that?"

PASSING THROUGH PROVIDENCE

"My harmonica," Rossi said.

"Can I buy one?" the boy asked him.

"Sure you can," he said.

"Where'd you get it?"

"At the music store."

Laurie came back with the girl.

"All set?" Rossi asked her.

"Yes," she said. "We're the best babysitters in town."

"Nothing but the best," he said, starting the bus down the road.

After they dropped off some kids, the children grew louder, so loud you couldn't hear the radio. It always happened when Alicia wasn't there. Rossi pulled the bus over.

"You're making too much noise," he said. "If you don't quiet down, I'll turn off the radio." The talking subsided to a whisper. "Good," he said, winking at Laurie, then continued his run.

Some days, driving around the streets of Providence was an adventure, because of all the construction projects. On windy days, the streets became obstacle courses with the empty trash cans rolling around and broken tree branches falling down.

He stopped at a corner and let some kids out, then they came to the Hartford Projects. Several kids left the bus at once and the noise was gone. Rossi smiled. "Glad to see them go," he told Laurie.

Finally they came to the last stop. One child left, little Joanna. He stopped and blew the horn at her house. They waited a few minutes and there was no sign of life. Laurie stepped from the bus, knocking on the front door of the house. "No one here," she shouted at Rossi.

He blew the horn some more.

"I just can't leave her here alone. She's too small," Laurie said.

Finally, the door opened. Her mother appeared in a bathrobe, looking like she was on drugs. "I'm sorry, I fell asleep," she said, taking the child.

Laurie climbed back on the bus. "You know," she said, "a lot of these kids don't have a chance to grow up. They just fall through the cracks."

"I know," he said.

When they returned to Turner Yard, he asked her if she wanted a ride home.

"You still have that old Ford Escort?"

"Sure do," he said.

"Okay, I'll wait for you," she said.

11
Bad Kids

In the afternoon, Eva Gomez went back to work feeling miserable. She was still upset with her husband and wasn't talking to him. She walked through the yard searching for her bus and couldn't find it, so she went to the office and told Kenny.

"Just a second," he said and checked a list of unit numbers. "Your bus is in the garage for maintenance, use spare eleven."

"My bus is always in the garage," she complained.

"Well, I can't help that," Kenny said.

She spun around, rushing outside and marching through several rows of buses. When she found number eleven, it had no key. She was breathing hard and getting upset. She searched everywhere for it and finally found it under the seat, then she had to get her special shoes from her car.

She climbed back on the bus, putting on her platform shoes. She adjusted the seat, pushing it all the way forward, so her feet could reach the accelerator. She started the engine, checking everything twice before turning on the radio to some Latino music; then she drove around to the monitor's side of the building, waiting for the manager to come.

"I got no one today," he told her.

"Thanks for nothing," she said.

"I'm sorry," he said.

Several minutes later, she turned onto the street next to the middle school. Another bus was waiting there and the driver was bald headed. He came over and introduced himself.

"My name is Boris. How you doing?" he said.

His English was good, but she knew he wasn't from this country.

"Where you from?" she asked him.

"Russia," he said.

"You have a monitor." She could see someone sitting in his bus.

"Yes," he said.

"So what are you doing in this country?"

"The same as you, trying to make a living," he said.

"Would you like to join my lottery pool? We have it every week."

"Okay," he said. "How much?"

"Three dollars. Maybe someday we'll be rich," she said.

"That would be nice," he said.

Soon the bell rang and the students came across the grounds like a human wave, loading onto the buses. Eva hated to do her run alone, because she knew the kids were more trouble.

"Where's the monitor?" a boy asked her.

"At home, where I should be," she said.

"All right!" the boy exclaimed. "No monitor today."

"Sit down and be quiet," she told them.

As soon as the buses were full and ready to go, a teacher gave the signal for them to leave.

She drove a few blocks down the road when the problems started. Kids were shouting and paper balls were flying through the air like snowballs, so she pulled over by the side of the road.

"Be quiet!" she yelled at them. "You better stop throwing things or you're going back to see the principal."

She drove a couple of more blocks. The noise continued to get louder. A boy was shouting the "F" word. Eva turned the bus around, heading back toward the school. Now the kids grew quiet.

"Don't go back," a girl said. "We'll be good."

"You should have listened to me before." She called Kenny on the two-way radio. "These kids are bad. I'm taking them back to school and I want the principal to meet the bus."

"Ten-four, I'm making the call," Kenny answered.

She returned to the school and waited for a couple of minutes, until the principal came.

"What's the matter?" he asked, getting on the bus.

"These kids are too much trouble," she told him. "They're throwing papers and saying bad words."

They were very quiet as the man stood facing them. "Do you want to graduate from this school," he asked, "or be left behind…" He paused for a minute. "I'm sure you don't want to lose your friends and be left behind. Now, tell me who's causing the trouble?"

"Those two boys." Eva pointed to them. "And that girl."

"All right, you three, let's go. I'm calling your parents to come and get you," he said. The three kids had long faces as they followed him into the building.

Eva was pleased as she drove away. The rest of the students remained quiet for about a mile down the road, then someone threw something that sailed over her right shoulder, hitting the dashboard, landing on the floor next to her. It was a big round condom inside a wrapper. There was a muffled laugh behind her.

"Rotten kids," she said.

12
The Russian

Boris Tolchek came to this country to make a better life for himself. Times were lean in Russia and unemployment was high. The people there could only afford the bare necessities. He wanted more.

For awhile, he was a deckhand on a container ship, working his way over to this country. Within a few years, he married a local girl and bought a house in Providence. He missed his mother and sisters, but he promised to call them on the phone. They were a happy family until his father died, leaving them with little savings and a small bakery, where they made just enough to survive.

Each month Boris managed to send them money, so they were able to buy flour to make the bread and rolls to sell. Long ago, he'd learned some English in school, but it wasn't enough. After coming to this country, he went to school nights learning enough to read the city newspaper.

He had a very odd sense of humor. Sometimes he played games with people's minds. One day when no one was watching, he opened all the windows in someone's bus in the pouring rain. He liked to have a good laugh, but when it came to money, he was dead serious.

After he finished his morning run one day, he took the bus to the lumberyard and bought some wooden boards. He put them through the back door onto the floor between the seats.

He drove home and unloaded the boards in his driveway. Mary, his wife, came outside when she heard the bus running. She was a big lady with shoulder-length brown hair and a happy face. She was always energetic and liked to talk.

"What are you doing?" she asked him.

"I'm going to build a porch onto the house when I get time."

"Oh, that's a good idea. If it gets hot in the summertime, we can sit outside and get some air."

He was taking off the last of the wood from the bus. "What's for lunch?" he asked. He was always hungry.

"Ham and cheese sandwiches," she said.

"Sounds good to me."

"Do they know you're using the bus?"

"Who?"

"Your company."

"If I don't tell them, they won't know."

"Oh, I see." She laughed.

He finished up and returned the bus to the yard, then drove his car home. Tomorrow he was going to do a charter on the sly.

13
Old Folks

Jack Miller was dreaming again. His mail bag was loaded on his shoulder, his back killing him. He was walking down endless streets, mile after mile, with a ton of letters to deliver. Mad dogs attacked him. He ran, getting away. They chased after him. The dogs turned into tigers with sharks' teeth....

Jack sat up in bed sweating, his heart pounding. It was just another nightmare. He wiped his forehead with his hand. His pension from the post office wasn't enough, he thought. He should be getting compensation for mental stress too.

His wife was sound asleep in bed. There was some Tylenol and water on the nightstand next to him. He took two tablets and a drink. He was having doubts about himself. Why couldn't he sleep normal? Was something wrong with him? Should he see a doctor? His credit card debt from gambling was still growing. He'd lost thousands and had to find a way to win it back.

One Saturday morning he had an easy charter. It was for an old folks' home. Pedro, the security guard, met him in the yard.

"Where you going?" Pedro asked him.

"For a joy ride," Jack said, trying to be funny. He was wearing his mailman sweater.

"Maybe you have some letters to deliver." Pedro grinned.

"I have to take some old people to Woonsocket," Jack said.

"Wooon-suck-it," Pedro said.

"What bus should I use?" Jack glanced around the yard.

"Take any one you want," Pedro said.

"I need one with fuel."

"Let me know when you're ready to go, so I can check you out," Pedro said.

There was a GMC in the front yard. He sat at the wheel, starting it up. The fuel gauge showed half a tank. It was enough to get him there and back. He gave the bus a quick inspection. Using the charter form, he wrote down the starting time and mileage, then swept the floor and was ready for the trip.

He pulled slowly forward, waiting at the gate. Pedro came and copied the unit number down on his clipboard. "Have a good day, Jack. You watch out for those crazy old ladies," he said.

It was early and the traffic was light. The senior home was located on the east side of Providence, off Blackstone Boulevard. It was a large building surrounded by huge green lawns and trees. Jack followed a two-lane road to the front door and parked. He placed a small wooden stool in front of the bus steps. It was used by old people, making it easier to get up to the door.

He sat and read a newspaper while he waited, trying to keep his mind off gambling. He chewed a stick of gum instead of smoking. Twenty minutes passed. He wondered if anyone was coming. He decided to go inside and look around. There was a lady standing behind a counter.

"Can I help you?" she said.

"I'm supposed to pick up a group of people for Woonsocket," Jack said.

"They should be right out," she assured him.

"Just checking," Jack said, going back to the bus.

Several elderly ladies finally came outside, walking slowly; they had to be helped up the steps.

"Is this everyone?" Jack asked.

"No, there's more coming," someone said.

A minute later another group of people came. Three men were among them. The ladies were in very good spirits, talking and laughing. They seemed happy to be going someplace.

"Are we ready?" Jack asked, counting fifteen passengers all together.

"You can go," a lady said. "Everyone is here."

Going through the east side, he drove the bus back onto the city streets. When he came to Route 146 East, he turned onto the freeway and maintained a speed of forty-five. Glancing into the rearview mirror, he could see a couple of the ladies watching him.

"Driver, do you have the time?" one of them asked him.

"Ten forty-five," Jack said, looking at his watch.

The passengers smiled, sat back, and enjoyed the ride.

Twenty minutes later he pulled over to the side of the road and stopped. The city of Woonsocket is less than thirty minutes from Providence, but for some reason it seemed farther. Behind the charter sheet was a map he studied. He wasn't sure about the streets. "Does anyone know how to get there?" he asked the group, hoping to get a positive answer. Everyone just looked at him with blank faces.

"You don't know where you're going," someone said.

"I'm not sure," Jack said, "but don't worry, I have written directions. I'm sure we'll find the place." He looked at the map again for a minute, before putting the bus in gear. He followed the directions and drove along, passing a shopping center with a supermarket, making a right turn at the second red light, going several blocks over a bridge, taking a left turn.

To his surprise, there was a boat waiting on the Blackstone riverbank. It was one of the few times he'd ever found a place by using a map.

"Here we are," Jack said proudly. The tour boat was tied to a wooden dock alongside a lazy river. There was a refreshment stand, ticket booth, and a port-a-john.

"You did a good job," a lady said, smiling as she stepped onto the sidewalk. The old people were happy to make it on time. They seemed amazed that Jack didn't get lost. The group made their way over to the boat.

He parked the bus in an empty lot across the street, before walking back to the river. He waved good-bye to the people as their boat floated away from the dock. He glanced up the street and saw a shopping plaza with a fish-and-chip restaurant.

He had nothing else to do, so he went to look, hoping he could get a cup of coffee. It was after eleven in the morning and he wasn't sure if he wanted lunch. He could smell the fish, so he went inside and saw a couple eating at one of the tables. The prices seemed reasonable and the smell was making him hungry.

"Can I help you?" the girl said behind the counter.

"I'll try the fish and chips."

Some more people came in while he was standing there. The counter girl quickly put his order together.

"Here you go," she said.

"Thank you," he said, paying her. He took a seat at a table and poured ketchup over his fries. The light brown battered dipped fish tasted good with tarter sauce. He never had fish so early in the day. What a change in diet, he thought.

After he finished, he slowly sipped a cup of coffee. Several minutes later he left, taking a free newspaper near the door. He went back to his bus and sat in the driver's seat, reading the paper. On one page there was an ad about the Indian Casino, free buffet, and coins with Gray Line Tours. While sitting there, he was thinking about the money he'd lost.

Suddenly a loud blast made him jump. It was the horn from the riverboat coming back. He started the bus and moved it across the street.

Soon the passengers came from the dock. One by one they hobbled up the steps. They greeted him and returned to their seats. They had to wait for a couple of people who were using the port-a-john.

Jack counted heads when everyone was back.

"Someone is missing," he said.

Everyone looked around.

"Did someone fall in the water?" he said.

Everyone's mouth fell open.

"Just joking with you," Jack laughed.

Everyone let out a sigh of relief.

He drove the bus away, going through the city, only slower this time. He felt that these people were in no hurry and had nowhere to go.

During the ride most of them were talking. A man was eating a banana and two ladies were playing cards. When he pulled in front of the retirement home and parked the bus, someone said, "We're back." Everyone thanked him and descended onto the sidewalk.

It was a nice easy charter. No noise and troublesome kids. One lady surprised him and slipped two dollar bills into his hand.

14
A Game of Pool

Every morning Lenny Harris did his regular run with the school of the deaf. The students were mostly quiet and used hand signals to communicate. The other drivers would sometimes tease him. "Hey Lenny, how can you stand the silence?"

"I just turn on the radio," he told them with a smile.

October came and each day he returned to Turner Yard with his empty bus, stopping just long enough to pick up the trainees. It was a boring routine and he would have rather been fishing somewhere.

"We're going to practice backing up," Lenny said, as they rode to Pleasant View School. "It's a very important part of the test. And you have to know how to do it."

When they came to the school, Lenny put two orange cones on the ground. "You have to back up between them," he said. "Then you have to stop the bus. If you hit any one of them, you might not pass."

He let the group practice for over an hour. They were slowly improving. While he was standing there smoking a cigarette, he was thinking about the money he needed for a car payment, before the loan company repossessed it. He thought about selling drugs for a minute, then he had an idea. He'd play the numbers for a couple of days. It was a long shot, but it was worth a try. He could get lucky. If he didn't, he might have to do something else, like rob a bank or who knows....

The trainees took turns backing the bus up between the cones.

"Lenny, how am I doing?" Ida, the black girl, asked him.

"You're doing real good," he said, walking around the outside of the bus to the front, where he popped open the hood. "Now we're going to do the pre-trip. You're first, amigo," he told one of the Hispanic men.

The group took turns for the next hour, naming the parts of the motor and everything associated with the bus. One guy, his English was so bad, it was hard to understand what he was saying.

"Everyone on the bus," Lenny said. "Someone has to drive."

After they were all seated, a guy took the wheel. He put the bus in gear, jerking forward, going faster.

"Slow down! What's the hurry?" Lenny said.

The guy drove slower around the parking area, until Lenny was satisfied. The other trainees each had a turn, before going back to Turner Yard.

On the way home that evening, Lenny stopped his car at the Pine Street Pool Hall. He went in to have a drink and play some numbers.

"Beer," he said, sitting at the bar.

"Tap or bottle?" asked the bartender.

"Tap." He liked his beer served in a glass.

There were four pool tables in one area. The place seemed dead. Lenny sat thinking about his situation.

Another black guy came from the men's room and started playing pool by himself at one of the tables. "Hey man, you wanna play a buck a game?" he said.

PASSING THROUGH PROVIDENCE

"Make it five and you're on," Lenny said. He was always good at pool.

"It's your money," the guy said. "I'm Pratt. Let's play."

Lenny went over to the rack and picked out a straight pool stick. He chalked the blue tip. "You go first."

"I'll flip you for it," Pratt said, letting a quarter fly into the air.

"Heads," Lenny said.

"Tails, you rack, man," Pratt said.

He put all the balls inside the rack, sliding it into position on the table, leaving the balls in a perfect triangle, before pulling the rack up.

"Break," Lenny said, sipping his beer.

The other man shot the white cue ball with his stick and scattered all the balls over the tabletop, but none of them fell into the pockets.

"You left it easy for me," Lenny said as he aimed his stick, shooting a ball into the pocket. He blew a shot on purpose, giving this guy a chance.

On his next turn, Pratt stroked a couple of balls into the pocket before he missed. Lenny sunk another one, then missed again on purpose. The other man knocked in the rest of the balls and won the game.

The guy wasn't that bad, but Lenny knew he was better. He pushed a five spot across the table. "Not bad, man," he said, as he racked them up again.

Lenny won the next game and continued to get better, winning several more times.

"That's it, man," Pratt said. "You're too good for me."

Lenny collected his money and had another beer. There was a lottery machine next to the cash register, so he gave the bartender some money and bought a fistful of tickets. He was hoping to make a killing.

On his way home, he drove his Caddy by a local bank. That's where the money's kept, he thought. He just wished he could get his hands on some.

It was getting dark and it started to rain. The cold droplets fell like tears. He turned on his windshield wipers and circled the block, going by the bank again. The building was closed for the night.

15
An Odd Charter

The sun was setting as Eva Gomez drove home from work. It had been raining earlier and black clouds lingered in the sky. She stopped her car at a corner store and ran inside to get a few things. She was paying the clerk when she saw Rossi. She knew him from the bus yard. He was wearing his sunglasses.

"How you doing?" she said, holding her bag of groceries.

"Just getting a few things," he said.

"I needed bread and milk," she said.

He followed her outside.

"Wow, look at that," Eva said.

There was a huge rainbow across the sky. It was spectacular, very wide and bright. People were stopping, gazing up.

"I haven't seen a rainbow in years," Rossi said. "It's awesome."

"Look at the colors," she said.

"Isn't it something," he said.

"I wish my kids were here," she said.

"Maybe it's an omen," he said.

"A what?"

"You know, a good luck sign."

"I hope so, I could use some luck," she said. "See you later."

That evening she cooked supper for her children. She had two girls and a boy. The boy, Miguel, was the oldest, born when she was only sixteen. He grew fast and was as tall as her.

Eva cooked them hamburgers, their favorite food. They could eat burgers every night and never complain, but if she made rice and beans, they would moan, "Not this stuff again, Mom."

"When I was a little girl in Puerto Rico, we were lucky to have rice and beans," she told them. "And we didn't go to school every day. Sometimes we had to work in the sugarcane fields."

"But Mom, that was a long time ago. Now everything's different," her son said.

"More burgers," her daughter said.

"You can have more," she said, "but you don't want to get fat."

She always made sure her children did their homework before going to bed. She still wasn't talking with her husband Luis. He was working the second shift at a factory and always came in late.

She kept busy that evening with a mountain of clothes to iron and didn't finish until midnight. Waiting for Luis, she lay down in bed to read a book and tried to stay awake, but her eyes became heavy and she fell asleep.

The next morning, she did her school bus run and came back to the yard. Kenny gave her an odd charter to the North Burial Grounds. This is loco, she thought. She read the sheet twice.

"Is this right? A cemetery?" she questioned him.

"That's right," Kenny said. "You know people are dying to get in there." He was trying to be humorous.

"Who would want to go there," she said, walking away.

At the Metropolitan High School, the students and teachers came out promptly, boarding her bus. Eva saw some big kids in the class; some of them even looked older than eighteen.

PASSING THROUGH PROVIDENCE

In a short time, she drove them across town to the gates of the burial grounds. She never liked cemeteries. The place was surrounded with a black cast-iron fence that gave her chills. She drove the bus through the entrance onto a narrow road that led into the site, passing ancient gravestones.

A teacher told her where to park. Numerous trees were growing there, and the grounds were littered with leaves and twigs. She hoped she wouldn't have to stay. The place gave her the creeps. Someone must have made a mistake, she thought. Her jaw dropped open when she heard the teacher.

"This is a unique experience for us. We can learn something today while we clean up the grounds. This is the oldest cemetery in the state, even Civil War veterans are buried here."

"They're going to work?" Eva said. The words just came out of her mouth before she could think, but she thought it was a good idea.

"What's that?" said a teacher.

She put her hand over the mouth.

"Yes, they're going to work," said the teacher.

The cemetery director came by, and he told them there were not enough workmen to keep up the grounds.

"I want to thank you students who came to help," he said. "I really appreciate it. You can walk around the cemetery and learn so much. There's a lot of history here."

Every student was given a plastic bag as they came off the bus and converged on the grounds. A workman armed the kids with rakes and other utensils. They scattered around the cemetery in groups; some of them raked leaves and papers into piles, while others filled the bags.

The students worked laboriously. Broken twigs and branches

were stacked neatly together to be picked up later. Filled bags were left mounded together in loading zones along the road. After a few hours, some of the kids grew tired and stood around talking with each other.

Eva was sitting in the bus. She had no intention of stepping outside and walking around dead people's graves. The thought of it made her nauseous. She put on the radio and listened to a talk show to keep her mind occupied.

Finally a teacher came to her, giving her the good news: they were done and would be leaving soon for a cookout at Goddard Park.

"Good job," the director thanked them as they boarded the bus. "If I had you kids every day, this place would be in excellent condition," he said.

Eva was glad to get on the road again.

16
A Rainy Day

Rossi's only company was his cat, Tommy Boy. He was bored with television and grew tired of reading books. He couldn't get Laurie out of his mind. He took her home from work a few times, stopping at a donut shop once for coffee. He liked her company, but he sensed something was wrong. He knew she liked to be independent and that she lived alone in a small apartment in Cranston. What he couldn't understand was why she married some guy she didn't know.

He hadn't seen her for a couple of days, so he tried calling her on the phone. There was no answer. He wondered where she went, did she disappear again? No matter what happened, he wanted her back. He laid on his couch, gazing out the window. There was no moon or stars that night, only darkness.

In the morning, a cloud of gray smoke hung over Turner Yard. Over a hundred buses were warming up and the exhaust fumes were so thick, it was like a fog. Rossi searched for his bus and couldn't find it. Frustrated, he headed for the office. Suddenly there was a bright flash of lightning. It started pouring and he was getting wet, so he ran to get inside the building.

"I can't find my bus," he told the dispatcher.

"Wait a minute," Kenny said, reading a maintenance repair

sheet. "Your bus is in the garage. I think I have one spare left. There's no number on the bus, so I'll give you the unit number." He quickly wrote it down on a piece of paper.

"Do you know where it's parked?" Rossi asked him.

Kenny thought for a moment. "I think it's by the railroad tracks."

Rossi went back outside in the rain. He was glad he was wearing a baseball hat—a little protection was better than none. He located the bus and started the engine. There was just enough fuel to complete a run. He turned on the heaters, hoping to get dry. One headlight wasn't working. It was the last spare bus, so he had to use it. He found a Boston station on the radio that played rhythm and blues. His toes were really burning from athlete's foot, so he stomped his feet down on the floor like an idiot.

The commuter train to New York flew down the tracks by the yard with six passenger cars in tow. The noise from the train only lasted a few seconds, then it was quiet again. He drove his bus into the line for a monitor and picked up Alicia. He glanced around for Laurie, hoping to see her, but she was nowhere in sight.

"We are getting so much rain," Alicia said.

"I know," Rossi said.

"You have a different bus today."

"Mine's in the garage."

"They must be fixing it," she said, putting on some black lipstick.

"I hope so," he said, driving away from the yard.

The windows were fogging up, so he turned on the defrosters.

"I should have stayed home today," she said.

"You can't make any money if you stay home," he said, trying to cheer her up. They were together about four hours a day, more than some married couples. She was very nice and several times she mentioned she had no boyfriend. Rossi never was interested, especially since he'd met Laurie again.

They came to their first stop. A group of students standing on the corner rushed into the bus to get dry. None of them had raincoats or umbrellas. There was a middle school on the street.

"Why can't these kids go there, then they wouldn't have to catch the bus," Rossi said.

"Maybe there's no room," Alicia said.

"I don't understand why they have to be bused all over town. I bet if everyone went to their local school, the city could save a fortune."

"You think so?" she said.

"With all the money they saved," Rossi continued, "they could build more schools." He drove to the next stop and everyone was there. He opened the door for them and wondered why so many kids came on rainy days; maybe their parents were glad to get rid of them. He could see JoVon Macky sitting behind him through the rearview mirror. The boy was wearing the same dark sweatshirt with the hood hanging over his head, hiding his face. A few kids had their eyes closed, trying to catch a nap. Easy Lucy was awake, chewing a big wad of gum. Another girl was eating a bag of chips.

"I don't see the Thomas twins," Rossi said.

"They were suspended again," someone said in back.

The rain stopped momentarily and left huge puddles of water everywhere. It wasn't long before he pulled the bus up at the middle school and let everyone out.

There was time to spare, so they went to McDonald's. Rossi liked to drink coffee on cold mornings. Alicia was hungry so she bought a breakfast sandwich. They sat in a booth and talked.

"You're not eating anything," she said.

"I'm not hungry," he said.

"That's why you're not gaining any weight," she said.

"Well, I just want coffee."

"Do you have a girlfriend yet?"

"No, but I'm working on it," he said.

"I see," she said. "Does she live around here?"

"She's a monitor."

"She is," she said, surprised. "What's her name?"

"Laurie Edwards."

"Laurie, I don't know her. What bus does she ride?"

"I'm not sure," he said. "She rides a different one every day."

The sun came out, shining between the clouds and the rain let up. They were back on the bus again, doing the elementary run. Coming to a house stop, he blew the horn and waited for the kid. The next corner, a Hispanic boy from the housing projects showed up for the first time in a week.

"How come you missed so many days?" Alicia asked him.

"Because my mother didn't wake me in the morning," he said.

Rossi and Alicia just looked at each other.

"That's not good," she said. "You have to go to school, that's the law."

"Does he take any meds?" Rossi wanted to know.

"Are you special ed?" she asked the boy.

"Yeah, my mother said I'm crazy so she can get a check every month," he told them.

Rossi just shook his head in disbelief.

Big Ben was throwing things in the back and saying bad words.

"What's wrong with you?" Alicia asked him. "Do you want to

see the principal?"

"I lost my money," he said with a sad face.

Rossi stopped at Charlie Simpson's house, blowing the horn. His mother opened the door, waving her index finger.

"He's not going," Alicia said.

"That's Crazy Eyes' house," a kid said, as the bus continued down the road.

Little Carlos let out a yell and started crying. Alicia went back a couple of rows to check on him. She took his hand and made him sit next to her. He was holding his hands over his face, weeping.

"What's the matter with him?" asked Rossi.

"Someone hit him and he won't tell me who," she said.

Arriving at the school, Rossi turned the radio up, waking everyone who was sleeping. "Let's go," he said. "Time for breakfast. Don't leave anything on the bus. Make sure you have your book bag and your shoes and socks."

Everyone was happy to leave, laughing when they heard the phrase "shoes and socks," except for Big Ben.

"What's the problem?" Rossi asked him.

"I lost my money," he said.

"Did you look for it?"

"I can't find it anywhere. Can you loan me a dollar for snack time?" he said.

"Do I look like a bank?" Rossi asked him.

"I'm gonna starve," Ben said with a sigh as he left the bus.

After letting Alicia off in Turner Yard, he found a space to park the bus. He checked the floor and found some crayons and pennies. Reaching under the seats, he saw something green. It was Ben's dollar, stuck between a crack. He would save it for the boy.

He went inside the building, where a few drivers were waiting for extra work. He punched his card and headed for his car.

Lenny Harris and his trainees were getting on a bus.

"There's a guy who has a real eye for the job," Lenny said, trying to be funny.

Rossi didn't pay him any attention and reached his car just before the rain came again. He slid into the seat behind the wheel and started it, driving up the road. He saw someone waiting to catch the city bus on Union Avenue. It was Laurie.

"Get in before you get soaked," he shouted out the window.

"Thanks, Ross." She opened the door, taking a seat.

"I tried to call you a few times, but there was no answer," he said.

"I wasn't home. I was staying at my brother's house for a few days." She took out a comb from her handbag and ran it through her dark hair.

"Were you sick or something?"

"More like sick and tired," she said

The rain was coming down so hard, he pulled off the road for a minute.

"I like the way you do that," he said, watching her.

"Do what?"

"The way you do your hair."

"Sometimes you're weird," she said.

"I just think you look nice, that's all."

"So why'd you call me?"

"I wanted to talk, you know, see how you were doing. I still don't understand why you got married."

"I'm sorry, Ross. Things just happened so fast. I really don't want to talk about it." She turned on the radio and put her comb away, lighting a cigarette. For the rest of the way, she smoked and listened to the music. He continued driving through the rain. She lived on a dead-end street in Cranston.

When he pulled up at her place, she invited him in for coffee. They went into the kitchen, where there were some appliances, a table, and chairs. She had to use the bathroom. From where he was sitting, he could see three rooms with little furniture. There was a twelve-inch television on the counter next to the stove. After a minute, she came back and made coffee.

"Small place you have here," he said.

"It's all I can afford." There were some dirty dishes in the sink, so she turned on the water.

"I have to wash these," she said.

"You need any help?"

"Of course not," she said, putting on an apron.

"You don't have too much furniture," he said.

"I have everything I need."

"Can you afford this place, working part-time?" he asked.

"Not really, sometimes I'm late paying the rent. One time they turned off my phone, but I manage."

He sat drinking his coffee until she finished with the dishes and sat down.

"So Ross, when are you going to buy a new car?"

"One of these days," he said.

"How's your cat? Do you still have him?"

"Yes I do."

"Just a second, I need a cigarette." She went looking for them in the other room. The phone rang. "Ross, can you answer that for me?"

He picked up the receiver. "Hello," he said. A man's voice was on the other end. "Yes, she's here. Just a minute. Laurie, it's your brother."

She came back and took the phone, talking for awhile.

"He just wanted to see how I was doing," she said. "I think he worries about me."

"I worry about you too," Rossi said.

"You do, really...?"

"Yeah, I'm afraid you're going to run off and disappear again."

"Oh, will you stop. I made a mistake." She exhaled the smoke from her cigarette and turned on the television, pretending to watch it.

"You know, I live alone. Would you like to come over sometime?" he asked her, trying to be nice.

"How about dinner at your place tonight?"

"Now you're cooking," he said, surprised.

"No, you're cooking."

"That's fine with me," he said, thrilled.

"If I remember right, your cooking's pretty good," she said.

"In more ways than one," he said and smiled.

"Now Ross." She laughed.

17
A Bus Fight

Fat Eddy, a new driver, was trying to get into his bus. The door was locked, so he bend down and tried to pull it open from the bottom. Getting nowhere, he started scratching his head.

Boris Tolchek was sitting in another bus laughing so hard, he was trying to catch his breath. Earlier, he was in Fat Eddy's bus and closed the door from the inside, then jumped out the back.

After pulling himself together, he did his bus run with Green Middle School. However, he wasn't laughing anymore, because the kids on his bus were too loud. When he stopped the bus at an intersection for the traffic, a boy stood up using the "F" word and started fighting with another boy. Boris called the dispatch.

"This is seventy-three, I have a fight on my bus!"

"Do you have a monitor?" Kenny asked him.

"No, just me."

One of the boys pulled a knife out.

"He has a knife!" Boris said. "I have to break it up."

"I'm calling the police," Kenny said.

Boris yelled at the boys and told them the police was coming, but they wouldn't listen and kept fighting. One of the boys was cut across the chest and bleeding. He stepped between them. "Now that's enough!" he shouted. "Sit down and be quiet." The bleeding boy sat down. "You better sit down, it's over," he told the one with the knife. The kid just stood there for a minute, smiling. "I said it's over, now give me the knife," Boris demanded.

Just then, the police pulled up. The officer jumped out of the car and came into the bus. "What's going on here?" he bellowed.

The boy quickly put the knife in his pocket and sat down.

"These two are fighting and he has a knife," Boris said.

"Give me the weapon," the policemen said. The boy reached into his pocket and gave it to him. "Now, you two are coming with me. Let's go." The boys followed the officer to his car and were taken downtown.

"Everything all right?" Kenny asked over the two-way radio.

"Everything's all right now," Boris answered.

He had a special charter to do that morning. A few weeks ago, he took some index cards and printed "bus-for-hire" on them with his phone number. He put them on bulletin boards in churches and supermarkets.

Now he was getting some business. A group of Jehovah Witnesses hired him to take them across town for a few hours to a meeting. They paid cash and it was easy money, except for one thing—they kept singing religious songs on the bus and gave him a headache.

He thought about starting his own bus company someday. He needed to buy two good used buses that were mechanically sound and have them painted any color but yellow. However, getting the money was the problem; he had to do more charters, anything to make a buck.

18
Maxed Out

It was Teachers' Day and there was no school. Jack had to borrow another five hundred dollars from a credit card. He was feeling lucky as he parked his car. He caught the shuttle bus and felt like he was going to win a million bucks. The casino was always busy inside with crowds of people, gambling zombies with no life.

After waiting, Jack managed to elbow his way to the front of a roulette table. He thought the minimum bet of ten dollars was too much and wished it was less, but there was nothing he could do about it.

He started with two hundred in chips, using a parley system. He was playing odd or even numbers, trying to win two bets in a row and hoping to hit a hot streak. Some dealers had a knack for spinning the ball, making it land on 0 or 00. Whenever this happened, he picked up his chips and left.

After playing for an hour, he was tired of standing. He was ahead a couple of hundred and knew he had to stop playing for his back had started to bother him. He left the roulette table and sat down at a slot machine, dropping in a few coins.

Right away he was ahead fifty bucks and the waitress brought him a drink. The jackpot was twenty-five thousand, which was nice if he could win it, but he didn't. He just kept putting coins in the machine until he lost every dollar.

He felt like he was stabbed with a sword. He needed to win thousands, but his luck was bad. His credit cards were maxed out and he was going down a long dark tunnel with no end in sight. His head was pounding, so he decided to leave. The ride back home was always longer.

There was a note on the kitchen table. His wife had gone to visit one of their daughters. Both of his kids were married. He couldn't believe how fast they had grown and how the years passed.

Dogs were barking. Gazing through the window, he saw a mailman walking up the road. The guy was carrying a heavy bag, loaded down like a pack mule. He remembered how hard it was on his back and legs. He was glad he took early retirement.

The next morning Jack thought he had a school bus loaded with wild animals. One kid was mooing like a cow and someone was doing Woody Woodpecker. He was driving along when a penny bounced off the back of the windshield.

"Did you see who threw that?" he asked the monitor.

"No see nothing," she said, not speaking much English.

He went to the next stop and picked up more kids. Something hit him in the back. It was another penny. He watched them through his rearview mirror and didn't see anyone suspicious. Most of the girls were talking and some of the boys were playing cards or video games. Nothing unusual, so he drove on down the road.

"Everyone remain seated," he said, when they came to the school. He walked toward the back seats, glancing at each kid with a stern face. He didn't know what to do and just wanted them to sweat a little. He knew someone was guilty.

"Okay, you can go," he said after a few minutes.

On the way back to Turner Yard, the front tire blew out. Jack called the dispatcher and gave his location. They were on a side road and there wasn't much traffic. He stepped outside to examine the flat. The tire still had good rubber and there was no nail in it. There was a dark line going around the inside of the tread and part of it was separated. It looked like a retread. No way, he thought, not on a school bus....

19
Like a Movie

In October, there were pumpkin sales on every corner. It was Halloween time and people were stocking up with candy. Rossi bought a newspaper from a milk store and sat in his car, searching through the pages for something to do with Laurie. He saw an ad for a haunted house attraction. That would be different, he thought. A story caught his eye about a man arrested for rape. His name was Rudy Smith. He remembered his tenant Sadie talking about her son Rudy, whom she hadn't seen in years. He wondered if they were related. Maybe he would check with the police station later.

He drove to Federal Hill to his favorite bakery, where he bought a cheesecake, some pepper sticks, and wine biscuits. He paid the woman and headed home. Along the way, he ate a wine biscuit. He just couldn't resist the sweet smell.

When he returned to his apartment, he took a knife and sliced a piece of cheesecake, carrying it down to Sadie.

She was all smiles. "Thank you very much," she said.

He didn't tell her about the story in the paper. He didn't need to worry her. Besides, he wasn't sure it was her son.

"You want some breakfast?" she asked him.

"No thanks, I have to go jogging this morning."

"Well, if you change your mind, let me know," she said, cracking two eggs for herself, dropping them into a frying pan.

PASSING THROUGH PROVIDENCE

He went back upstairs and fed Tommy Boy and changed his water. He knew the cat liked fresh cold water, then he started getting things ready for dinner with Laurie. He took some chicken cutlets from the freezer to defrost. He checked his sauce and ziti, making sure he had enough. The sun was shining through the window.

"Look, Tommy Boy, the sun," he said. The cat jumped up onto the windowsill, sitting in the warm light. "What a smarty you are."

He changed into his gray sweat suit and hurried outside. When he was young, he was on the high-school track team and running was in his blood. Everything was drying up from the rain earlier, except the trees were still dripping wet. There were puddles in the street, so he jogged on the sidewalk.

A fast car came by and splattered water everywhere, just missing him. He didn't exercise every day, sometimes, he was just too tired. He ran down to Mount Pleasant High School and back home, about a mile, finishing with some jumping jacks.

In the afternoon, he was in his bus waiting for the kids. He was thinking about Laurie when the school bell rang. It was like a movie…lights, camera, and action. The characters came out of the building, getting onto the bus. Everyone was on stage now. Easy Lucy pushed a boy who was calling her names. Another kid was sneaking a drink of her soda. A boy opened a window, yelling at his friends on the sidewalk, showing them a picture of a naked lady. "Is this your sister?" he laughed.

Alicia, who was standing outside, came on the bus with someone new. She was checking his bus pass, talking to him in Spanish.

"He's from Guatemala," she told Rossi. "He doesn't speak English."

"If he doesn't know the language, how can he go to school?"

Rossi said.

"They have a special bilingual class," Alicia said.

"Until he learns English," Rossi said.

"Yes, until he learns," she said.

"Most of the kids don't know how lucky they are to be in this country," he told Alicia.

"Hey man, turn up the radio," someone said.

"You get what I mean?" Rossi said, putting the music louder. "Let's rock and roll." He stepped on the gas pedal.

When they finished that afternoon, he was supposed to meet Laurie in the parking lot. He sat in his car and waited, wondering if something went wrong. Several minutes later, she came walking along.

"Ross, I got stuck on a long run," she said, opening the door.

"I was getting worried," he said.

"I hate those long runs," she said.

"We're still having dinner at my place, right?" he said.

"Sure," she said.

He drove to his house and started cooking. It was easy for him to prepare a meal. Fish and chicken dishes were his favorite. To get things going, he opened a bottle of red wine.

"You want a drink?"

"Sure," she said.

He poured two glasses, then returned to the kitchen. The chicken cutlets were sizzling in the pan. Minutes later, he served them with pasta and sauce.

"That was fast," she said.

"Just like old times," he said, sitting down. They held up their glasses and drank. "And guess what we have for dessert?"

"I give up," she said. "What?"

"Cheesecake."

"Oh Ross, you remembered what I like. Why did I ever leave you?"

"Because I'm no fun."

"Oh yes you are," she said.

"How's the chicken?" he asked her.

"Delicious," she said.

The cat came over and made his presence known.

"I think he's hungry," she said.

"Here, Tommy Boy." He put a few pieces of chicken on the floor.

They had more wine after dinner. Later, he put the dirty dishes in the sink, then turned on the radio with some music.

"C'mon, let's dance." He took her hand, leading her to the living room. They slow danced for awhile. His body moved closer to hers, his hands caressing her back. "I missed you," he whispered, kissing her softly on the mouth.

After dancing, they sat on the couch.

"I need to rest. I think I ate too much," she said, lighting a cigarette. Before long, he was kissing her again on the neck. She pulled away for no reason. Suddenly, she started crying.

"What's the matter, Laurie?"

"Nothing, I just feel so happy being with you," she said.

"Here, take this." He gave her a tissue.

"Thanks," she said, wiping her eyes, then she went to the bathroom.

He watched the television and wondered what was wrong with her. She seemed upset for some reason. Why, he didn't know.

20
The Farm

Lenny Harris had no training class that morning and was given a charter for Sackett Elementary School. With an hour to spare, he took the bus downtown and parked near the police station. He never felt right with the police around and today was no exception. He wanted to see his buddy and entered the building.

"I'd like to talk with Rudy Smith," he told the desk sergeant.

"And you are?" the officer said.

"Just a friend," Lenny said.

"He's going to need a lot of friends," the officer said.

"Well, I'd like to talk with him and see how he's doing," Lenny said.

"Follow me," the officer said, leading him to a special room for visitors. "You sit there until he comes. You have five minutes."

He was on one side of a wall, looking through a thick plastic window like a bank teller. His buddy came in and appeared on the other side.

"How you doing, man," Lenny said.

"I'm innocent," Rudy said, looking worried.

"You need a lawyer?"

"I got a lawyer, but I didn't rape anyone. They got the wrong guy," Rudy said.

"I hear you, man. If you need anything, just let me know."

PASSING THROUGH PROVIDENCE

"Tell my friends I didn't do it."

"Okay, man," Lenny said.

"When I get out, I'm going to join the army and get the hell away from here."

"That's crazy, you're too old for the army."

"Then, I'll join the Salvation Army."

"Now you're talking."

After seeing his buddy, Lenny drove to Sackett Elementary School with the bus. He felt bad for his friend and wondered if there was anything he could do. The sky was blue and it was a good day for a field trip. He didn't like doing charters and taking a load of kids someplace wasn't his idea of fun, but he really needed the money to make a car payment. He tried playing the daily numbers several times and didn't have any luck. He knew he had to come up with a lot of cash soon.

When the children came, they were escorted by a teacher. Their small faces were from every race of life, and they were noisy little chatterboxes. They were filled with excitement and happy to be going someplace. Some of them had never left the city and didn't know what to expect from the trip. A few teachers came along with some parents.

Lenny waited until everyone was seated on the bus, then he adjusted his sunglasses and started down the road. He drove a few blocks before getting onto Route 95 heading south.

It wasn't long before they were passing cows in the pasture. They went by some trees in the woods that had the same colors as the kids' faces on the bus—red, brown, and yellow. It was a beautiful sight.

Approaching the farm, they went from the clamor of the city

to the calm of the country. There were endless fields of vegetation ready to be harvested, rows of golden corn and green beans. Lenny could see for miles in either direction, nothing but earth and sky. How nice it would be to live out here, he thought.

However, when the kids saw the farm, the tranquility didn't last long. They were loud and anxious to get out. A teacher had to quiet them down.

Lenny pulled behind a row of school buses already waiting. A guide lady came and gave him directions. He drove slowly, following a dirt road around a building to the other side where they parked. The kids, loud again, were jumping in their seats. Some of them acted like they had never been anywhere in their lives.

An old farm building stood on the land with a produce stand. There was a display of fruits and vegetables; even homemade pies and muffins were for sale. A few people were buying bags of apples.

When the bus was empty, Lenny sat there resting his ears. He felt tired and lightheaded, for he'd had nothing to eat all morning. He stretched his legs outside, walking over to the open market. Next to the pie counter, he found a coffeepot. They had paper cups, so he filled one for himself, adding cream and sugar. The cashier told him it was free for bus drivers. He thanked her and bought a muffin. Outside, he met a Haitian driver who didn't speak very much English. The guy wanted to know where the toilet was located. Lenny pointed him to the other side of the building.

He made his way back to his bus and ate his muffin. Resting in his seat, he could see a tractor moving in the distance. It was pulling a trailer load of kids on a hayride. He watched another bunch of kids going through a giant corn maze. He finished his coffee and was feeling better now that he had something to eat. He lit a cigarette and strolled around the bus, checking the tires.

After an hour, the children came back and sat at the picnic tables in the area. The teachers passed out lunches and everyone ate. They played horseshoes and games for awhile, then they all had to use the bathroom.

When it was time to leave, each kid was given a gift from the farm. They came back on the bus smiling and carrying orange pumpkins. A teacher was missing, so they had to wait. Finally, she came from the produce stand with a bag full of fruit. The kids were singing, "Old MacDonald had a farm…." Lenny couldn't wait to get the bus on the road.

21
A Bus Fire

The yellow bus crawled up the hill, the engine sputtering. Eva Gomez was driving it. She was taking kids home from school when some black smoke started coming from the dashboard. She pulled over and quickly called the dispatcher.

"Emergency," she said. "I think something is burning. I see smoke."

"How bad is it?" Kenny asked.

"The smoke is getting bad," she answered. "I think it's on fire."

"Evacuate the bus! Get the kids out right away!" Kenny told her. "I'm calling the fire department. Give me your location."

"I'm on Parade Street, near the armory," she said.

"I copy, Parade Street. Now get the kids out!" he said.

She had the monitor lead the children onto a grassy field, about fifty yards from the bus. Eva turned off the key and followed them to the field. One boy was crying, "Where's my sister? She's not here!"

"Is she on the bus?" Eva said, alarmed.

The boy nodded his head. "Yes, she was sleeping."

Just then red flames shot up from the engine.

"Oh my God!" Eva said, running back to the bus. She hurried up the stairs and searched the seats. Her eyes started to burn from the smoke. She found the girl, still sleeping, and picked her up. She couldn't believe the child was left behind. She carried her outside and raced across the grass.

The firemen were on the scene in minutes. The front of the bus was completely engulfed in flames with smoke going up to the sky. The men sprayed a sheet of white foam over the fire until the flames died and smothered out. It didn't take long.

Linda Stevens, the manager, came in her car from Turner Yard. She inspected the damage, calling for another bus on her cell phone. A fireman talked with them, asking some routine questions. Linda filled out a report on her clipboard.

"Are the children all right?" she asked.

"Everyone is okay," Eva said.

"Another bus should be here soon," Linda said.

"I need one with a block of wood on the gas pedal," Eva told her.

"Oh, I forgot, you have short legs." Linda called the dispatcher again.

Eva joined the monitor, staying with the kids. They sat watching as the firemen checked the bus, making sure the fire was completely out before they left.

An empty bus pulled up later with the driver. "It's all yours," the man said, before joining Linda in her car. Eva loaded the children into the bus and continued down the road.

Sunday morning, she took her three kids with her to church. They were dressed in their best clothes and happy to go. After Mass they went to a diner for breakfast. She told them about the fire on her bus. They were sitting at a table waiting for the waitress. Luis had to work late the night before, so he stayed home asleep.

"Was it a big fire, Mommy?" her son wanted to know.

"It was very bad, but the firemen put it out," Eva said.

The four of them sat next to a large window where they could see the traffic in the road.

"What are you having to eat, Miguel?" Eva asked him.

"I want the pancakes and bacon with orange juice," he said.

"Me too, me too," his little sisters said.

The waitress came and took their order, then she brought their drinks. Eva had coffee while she waited. Every Sunday they sat there and talked, gazing out the window. Her kids loved the pancakes.

On the way home she bought a Sunday paper. She liked to cut the coupons for the store. Her husband's car was missing from the driveway.

"I see your father's gone," she said.

She made some coffee and sat with the paper in her lap. She was looking for the page with the lottery numbers so she could check them. Every week she had Power Ball tickets from her pool at work. Most of the time they won less than twenty dollars, and today was no different.

She noticed yesterday's number was 6-1-8. Her heart skipped a beat; that's what she had played! She couldn't believe it. She looked at the number again and was ecstatic. She won over two hundred dollars.

"I won!" she said, blessing herself. "Thank you, Lord." She kissed the crucifix that hung around her neck. Her kids came from the other room when they heard her.

"I won some money," she told them.

"Can I have a new bike?" her son asked.

"I want a dolly," her daughter said.

"Me too, Mommy," her other daughter insisted.

"You kids have to wait until I get the money," she told them.

"Don't tell your father anything. I want to surprise him when he gets home."

"We won't tell," her son promised.

"Go play for now. I'll buy you something later," she said, pouring another cup of coffee. She intended to get something nice for herself too, maybe a new dress.

22
A U.S. Citizen

Boris Tolchek was still doing charters on the sly. He thought nothing of using the company bus and fuel. He only thought of the money he was making, up to five hundred a week. Dozens of buses left the yard each day for real-time charters and kindergarten runs. It was hard for anyone to keep track of them.

He was still sending money home to his mother each month so she could run the bakery. Once, he received a letter from her thanking him, letting him know how well she was doing and about how bad things were in Russia. People were still without work and no food.

Boris never told his wife about his bank account; he was waiting for the right moment. In time, he became fascinated with the stock market. He bought shares in companies like Apple and Dell. Some of his stocks split two for one, then went up again. He couldn't believe how fast his money was growing. Some of them went up to a hundred. He bought newspapers about stocks and studied the charts and read everything he could about the companies.

His wife Mary liked to go to the movies, so each week he took her to a dinner and a show. They went to a restaurant close to home that served good meals for less than ten dollars a person. While eating, he tried to tell her about his investments and the stock market.

"I think my Apple shares are going to a hundred," he told her.

"You really think so." She liked to eat, and cleaning her plate was no problem.

He kept talking about the stocks, then told her about his business plans.

"If I make enough money, I'm going to start my own bus company."

"Really?" She had her doubts. "Do you have any money saved?"

"Yes, I have been saving my money," he said.

"How much do you have?"

"I think I have enough to buy a bus. I'll get one to start, then later another." He kept talking and didn't shut up until they came to the show.

The following week, he was going to become a US citizen. After some loving one morning, he rolled out of bed and Mary made him breakfast.

"Today's your big day," she said.

"I don't know what to wear," he said.

"You have to wear a suit."

"I know, but which one?"

"You look good in brown, wear that one."

"I think I look good in anything."

"You sure do." She gave him a kiss.

He finished eating his home fries and eggs, then took a shower and dressed.

Mary was going with him. She wore her pantsuit and looked lovely with her long hair over her shoulders.

The sun was shining and it was almost eleven o'clock in the

morning. He found a place to park in the street. There were hundreds of people at the Veterans Auditorium in Providence. They were all going inside.

Boris and his wife followed everyone into the building. The lighting inside was dim and the air was stale. He had to sit in one of the rows closer to the front with a lot of other people. Mary sat in back with the family members.

Everyone there waited for awhile and was getting restless. Finally, the mayor came on stage and gave a long speech with a little history of America. When he finished, the judge came and talked, then everyone had to stand and raise their right hand while he gave them the oath, repeating the words after him.

"Congratulations," the judge said when they finished, "you are now US citizens."

Everyone applauded and shook hands.

23
A Handicapped Bus

Jack Miller was feeling terrible; his back was aching again from arthritis. He had to drive a handicapped bus because the regular driver was sick. He was supposed to have two monitors for the chair lift, but they were short-handed and he only had one. He had to help operate the lift and bring the wheelchair kids aboard. There were only eight kids all together; six of them sat in seats. A big Asian girl with a plump face, who wore a harness, had to be buckled to her seat. For most of the trip she kept saying, "Oh my God! Oh my God!"

"I wonder what's wrong with her," Jack said.

"She's having her period," the monitor said. "I know because, her mother told me."

"I had to open my big mouth," Jack said.

Along the way, one of the wheelchair kids kept slapping himself in the face. Another kid was jerking his head up and down, until he vomited on the floor.

"He's sick," Jack said, pulling over to the side of the road.

"He's not sick," the monitor said, throwing newspapers over the mess. "He does this every day, on purpose."

"Look," the boy said, pointing at the mess as if he was boasting, then he started laughing. "Look," he said again, pointing and laughing.

A shoe flew through the air, just missing Jack's head.

"Who threw that?!" Jack snapped.

"It was Jose. He always takes his shoes off. Sometimes he takes his clothes off too," the monitor said.

"What a zoo," Jack said.

When they came to the school, attendants were there to help. Everyone was unloaded except one boy. He sat on the floor of the bus and wouldn't move. After a few minutes, one of the men talked him into leaving by bribing him with a new video game to play.

Upon returning to Turner Yard, Jack brought the bus behind the building. He had to wash the floor with the water hose. "Man, this stinks," he said. "I'll be glad when the regular driver gets back."

He went home later and took some Tylenol for his back pain. The mail was still on the table from yesterday. He checked through the letters. One was from a bank, which he opened and found a new credit card. It came with a five-thousand-dollar credit limit and was like a gift from heaven.

He sat in his easy chair, thinking about going to the casino. Maybe his luck would change. His wife left early and wasn't home; she always had somewhere to go. He wanted to tell her about all the money he'd lost, but he didn't know how. He turned on the television for awhile and fell asleep.

24
Bus Monitors

It was Halloween and some monitors called up sick. They didn't want any tricks played on them by the kids. Most of the monitors were immigrants because no one else wanted the job. There were only a few Americans willing to do it, and some older people who needed the extra money.

Laurie Edwards was smoking a cigarette while she waited outside the building for a school bus. She used to work in a factory, but going to work early and returning home late at night was too much for her. She felt like she was on a merry-go-round, going in circles to work and home. She'd much rather deal with obnoxious kids for a paycheck. Anyway, it was a city job and the benefits were the best. She received full health insurance and paid sick days.

She was in her late thirties when she met her ex-husband. He wined and dined her for a couple of days and after too much to drink, he begged her to marry him. She knew she wasn't getting any younger, so she said yes.

Standing there, she felt lightheaded and nauseous. I have to stop smoking, she thought. She dropped the cigarette and stepped on it. Feeling dizzy, she leaned against the building, taking a couple of deep breaths. She wondered if she was catching the flu; some of the other monitors were sick from it.

"Are you feeling all right?" another woman asked her.

"I think so," she said.

"You have no color, your face looks white."

"Maybe I'm getting the flu," she said. A bus pulled up for her. She climbed in and sat down, hoping to feel better.

"Hello," the driver said, "I'm Eva."

"I'm Laurie," she said. "What time do you get done?"

"Four o'clock," Eva said. "Why?"

"That's good," Laurie said. "I have to catch a ride later.

They went a few blocks, going slowly by another school bus. It was parked by the side of the road with its hazard lights flashing. The monitor was waving her arms for them to stop. Eva pulled over.

"Is there a problem?" she asked the monitor. She could see the bus was loaded with noisy kids.

"My driver left, he's gone."

"What do mean, he quit?"

"The kids are bad, so he left. He said he wasn't coming back."

"Just a minute, I'm calling the dispatcher," Eva said. "Kenny, we have a problem."

"Go ahead, I'm listening," he answered.

"We have a bus load of kids here with no driver. The monitor said he quit."

"Where are you?" Kenny asked.

"Webster Avenue, near McDonald's."

"Okay, you tell the monitor to stay on the bus. I'm sending a spare driver right away."

"I'm telling her," Eva said. She leaned out the window. "The dispatcher is sending another driver. You'll have to wait."

"Wait, how long?" the monitor asked.

"It shouldn't be long. I have to go now." She continued on

her way.

"Can you believe that?" Eva said to Laurie. "He just quit."

"Did you hear those kids yelling on that bus? No wonder he quit," Laurie said.

Eva drove to a Catholic school in Cranston. It was next to a large cemetery. She stopped behind two other buses.

"Is this your regular run?" asked Laurie.

"No, I'm just doing it today because the driver is sick."

Laurie felt a little better, but she was still afraid of getting sick. She opened a window and stayed in her seat, combing her hair.

It wasn't long before the students came, carrying their book bags. They were all wearing school uniforms. Laurie thought some of the girls' dresses were too short. She counted sixteen boys and girls. A boy started cursing at a girl for some reason.

"Shut the hell up," the girl told him. The boy thumbed his nose at her.

"You both better shut up," Laurie said.

It was a cloudy afternoon as Eva drove back to Providence. She planned on going shopping later.

The girl and boy started mouthing off again. The boy gave her the finger.

"Asshole," the girl said.

"This is a Catholic school. I don't want to hear any filthy language," Laurie said, raising her voice. "I think you better sit up front," she told the boy.

"She's calling me names. Why do I have to move? I didn't do anything," the boy said.

"If you don't move, I'll have to sit next to you. You won't like that."

"Okay," the boy moaned, changing seats. He gave the girl the finger again.

"I'm going to have the driver stop right in front of your house. Then I'm going to tell your mother what you're doing," Laurie told him. "Would you like that?"

The boy's face turned red and he didn't say anything else. His stop came first. As the bus pulled away, he stood on the sidewalk, sticking up his middle finger.

25
Trick or Treat

The Hartford Projects on Halloween was like a war zone. Before driving the bus through, Rossi made sure all the windows were closed. He was taking the elementary kids home from school. They had a classroom party and some of them were still dressed in costumes. Everyone had candy.

"Boy, are they hyped up," Rossi said.

"I don't want to see anyone eating on this bus," Alicia told them.

No one was listening to her. Big Ben put another handful of candy into his mouth.

"Ben, did you hear me?" Alicia looked at him. "Do you want me to take your candy away?"

Ben swallowed a mouthful. "No," he said.

Little Carlos was moving around too much.

"Carlos, you come and sit with me." She made him come forward.

Charlie Simpson, with his good eye watching her, stuck a piece of bubble gum into his mouth.

There was a car accident on Hartford Avenue. The police were directing traffic around it. A crowd of people gathered on the sidewalk. Rossi had to go a different way.

Splat! Something hit the windows. Splat! Splat!

"He's throwing eggs at the bus!" Ben shouted.

A tall kid was standing on the curb, laughing. The eggs slid down the side of the bus, making a real mess. Rossi was glad the windows were closed.

"This happens every Halloween," Alicia said.

"I'd like to smash an egg in his face," Rossi said, but there was nothing he could do. He drove down the road and something else hit the bus.

"What was that?" Carlos asked.

"Someone's throwing rocks," Alicia said.

Rossi only had a few more stops to do. When he finished, he checked the windows of the bus and none of them were broken.

He picked up Laurie later, taking her to Mama Roses for dinner. It was a family restaurant where the food was like homemade. He had been there before and knew the service was good and prices were reasonable. They sat at a table for two and the waitress gave them menus, then she brought two glasses of water and a basket of sliced Italian bread.

Laurie liked shrimp scampi, so that was what she ordered. Rossi was having the baked stuffed fish. They sat across from each other, talking.

"I remember this place," she said. "Didn't we eat here?"

"Yes, we did," he said.

"Something smells good," she said.

"I hope you're hungry."

"I'm starving." She buttered a slice of bread and chewed on it.

They talked awhile longer and lost track of the time, then the waitress came with their meals.

"This looks good," Rossi said.

PASSING THROUGH PROVIDENCE

More people came into the restaurant and were seated. The place was getting busy.

"This shrimp is delicious," Laurie said.

"I'm glad you like it," he said.

"How's the fish?" she asked him.

"Very good," he said.

It was almost dark when they came outside.

"Thank you, Ross," she said, getting into the car.

"I'll be right back," he said. He crossed the street to a small store, buying a jug of milk and a few scratch tickets.

When he returned, he gave her the tickets.

"For me?" She seemed surprised.

"Maybe you'll get lucky," he said.

She rubbed off the spots. "I won twenty dollars!"

"See, I told you."

"Thanks, Ross. I can use the extra money."

On Halloween night, the kids were running through the streets, filled with exhilaration. "Trick or treat!" they shouted while carrying their bags. Rossi drove to his house and led Laurie inside. She sat on the couch in the living room and lit a cigarette, while he made coffee in the kitchen. She turned the television on and there was a horror movie showing.

He came with two cups of coffee, sitting them down on a small table, then he sat next to her. "It's a creepy movie," she said, "real scary." It was about werewolves. He put his arm around her and she rested her head on his shoulder. He started stroking her hair.

"It's real bloody," she said.

"Don't be afraid," he said, giving her a light kiss on the neck. She responded by kissing him on the mouth. This was like a green light for him. They fell on the floor and he unbuttoned her blouse, then they made love late into the night.

In the morning, she rushed from the bedroom to the bathroom and threw up. Rossi sat in bed and could hear crying.

"What's the matter?" he asked, concerned.

"I'm all right," she answered, wiping her tears and coming back to bed.

"Is something wrong?"

She started turning white.

"What's wrong, Laurie?"

"I think I'm pregnant," she finally said.

He knew something wasn't right.

"You really think so?" he said.

"I'm pretty sure, I missed my last period and now I'm spotting.

"So it's your ex-husband's baby?"

"What do you think, of course it's his," she said.

"You know, you could always get an abortion."

"I know, but I've been thinking. If I'm having a baby, I want to keep it, because I'm not getting any younger. This is probably my last chance."

"Then let me help you." He pulled her into his arms, holding her close. "We can raise the baby together."

"Should I tell my husband?"

"You mean, your ex-husband," he corrected her. "Why bother, he's still in jail and you're getting a divorce, so he doesn't need to know."

"It takes extra money to raise a baby," she said.

"I know, and I can help you. We really don't need two apartments either. You can move in with me."

She seemed relieved and held him close, hoping everything would be all right.

26
A Piece of Cake

The holidays were coming soon. It was November and Lenny Harris was broke. He was still behind on his car payments and paid another three hundred dollars for repairs. He tried to get a loan, but his credit was bad. His Caddy was everything to him. It was like his left arm, he couldn't exist without it.

He parked his bus near an alley. There was a trash dumpster next to a fence, where he hid a bike earlier. Now he was putting his plan into action. He rode the bicycle nonchalantly along the road and stopped at the bank.

Wearing his dark glasses and a black baseball cap, he went through the door. Three people waited ahead of him as he stood in line. Looking around, he didn't see a security guard anywhere. He pulled the front of his cap down and approached the teller. He gave her a piece of paper that said, *I have a gun pointing at you. Be nice and give me all your big bills, or I'll shoot you*. She read it, then her face turned pale and her hands started to tremble. Lenny glanced around. No one was watching him.

"Hurry up! I don't have all day," he told her.

She put a pile of bills on the counter without saying a word. He took the money before anyone noticed and stuffed his coat pockets.

"You have any more fifties or hundreds?" he asked her.

She shook her head in disbelief.

"Thank you." He blew her a kiss and walked away.

He went outside and hopped on the bike, pumping the pedals as fast as he could. He shot down the street like a rocket with his heart beating like crazy. He turned into the alley and flew through the last fifty yards, stopping at the dumpster. He pulled a handkerchief from his shirt pocket, wiping his fingerprints from the handle grips, then he left the bike hidden in the trash and headed for the bus.

He slid onto the driver's seat and changed his hat and glasses. Not seeing anyone around, he started the bus and drove away. Two police cars sped by with their lights glaring. He continued on down the road. "A piece of cake," he said to himself as he returned to Turner Yard.

That evening he went to the loan company and made the payments on his car. He wanted to celebrate, but couldn't tell anyone why. He thought about seeing Carmella; she was still angry at him over another woman. He stopped at a drugstore to get her something nice. She liked candy, so he bought her a box of chocolates. If she didn't want them, then he would give them to someone else.

27
Icy Conditions

Eva started her bus, turning on the radio to hear the news. It was a cold morning and the temperature had dropped below freezing. The weatherman said there were several accidents in the city due to icy roads. While she waited for the bus to warm up, she sipped a cup of coffee from the driver's lounge. The defrosters were on, clearing the windshield so she could see.

Before she could go, she had to clean the side mirrors with an ice scraper, then she drove the bus around to the line where a couple of other buses were waiting. She had to go solo again, for no monitors were available.

The roads were slippery and the traffic was slow. She was already running late. A signal light turned red, changing from green to red without flashing yellow. She hit the brakes and the bus slid right into the middle of the intersection.

"Oh my God!" she said, her heart pumping faster. She was lucky no one was coming the other way. For the next few blocks she was more cautious.

"Attention all drivers!" Kenny said over the two-way. "The streets are icy. Make sure you drive careful. If you're running late, don't worry about it."

I have to go slow, she thought to herself. There was an accident in the road, two cars crashed into each other. She made several stops; the kids were all there waiting. She continued along and could feel the bus slide when she went around a corner.

"How come you're late?" a kid complained to her.

"The roads are bad," she said. "Can't you see?!"

After leaving the kids at school, she checked the empty bus and found fresh graffiti on the seats.

"Loco kids," she said. Inside the empty bus she kept a bottle of Pine Sol in the overhead compartment. Using a rag, she cleaned everything.

After she finished and was parked in Turner Yard, she walked near the drivers' lounge and saw two police cars on the street with a small crowd of people gathered around them. Pedro, the security guard, was there.

"What's the matter?" she asked him.

"A kid's mother beat up the monitor, because her kid was suspended off the bus," Pedro said.

"That's terrible," Eva said.

"I know," he said.

"So the monitor is telling everything to the police," Eva said.

"Yes, she's filing charges against the mother," Pedro said.

"Good for her," Eva said. Later, she went inside to the bathroom.

On the way home, she stopped at a local market to get something for dinner, buying some chicken and hamburger. The man behind the meat counter was from Puerto Rico and was very helpful. He weighed up her order and packaged it. She didn't see too many customers in the store.

"So, how's business?" Eva asked.

PASSING THROUGH PROVIDENCE

"Not too good," he said, "the roads are bad because of the weather."

"Maybe you'll do better later."

"I hope so," he said.

She thanked him and put the packages in her cart. At the fruit section she picked out a cantaloupe and a bag of apples. One row was loaded with imported canned goods from south of the border. She put a couple of items in her cart, going around to the other side, when she spotted her husband. He was standing down in a corner talking with another woman. The lady was smiling.

Eva wondered what they were saying, moving her cart closer to hear them. Luis didn't see his wife until the last second, then the expression on his face changed.

"Hi honey," Eva greeted him.

"This is Maria. She works with me at the company," said Luis.

"I thought you were home sleeping," Eva said.

"I was awake early, so I came to the store to buy some cigars, then I saw Maria," he said.

"I'm getting groceries for us. Can you help me carry them to the car?" Eva went to pay the cashier. She could have carried the bags herself; she just wanted to get her husband to follow her.

Before leaving the woman, Luis whispered something to her.

"You bought cigars, but I never see you smoke them," Eva said.

"I smoke at night when I'm working," he said, annoyed. "I have to go now."

"Where are you going?" she asked.

"To change the oil in my car," he said.

She went home unhappy. She wished her husband would spend more time with her and the children. She carried the groceries into the house and thought about the woman in the store. Luis said she worked for his company. Did he really go change the oil or was he lying?

Several drivers were sick in the afternoon, and Linda Stevens was begging everyone to work extra hours. Eva had a headache and didn't feel like driving, but they really needed her. They even gave her a monitor.

She was parked at an elementary school, sitting behind the steering wheel of the bus, watching the kids come up the steps. The monitor, a large black lady, was outside talking to someone on the sidewalk. A Hispanic boy came on the bus crying and his face was covered with blood. He was small, about six years old, bleeding from his mouth and nose. Eva gave him some tissues to wipe the blood.

"What happened to you?" she asked the boy.

"A big kid beat me," he sniffled.

"Do you know his name?"

"No" was all he could say.

Eva blew the horn to get the monitor's attention and pointed to the bloody boy.

"What happened to him?" she asked.

"He got into a fight," Eva said. "I think you should take him to the nurse."

"What if she's not there?"

"Then leave him in the principal's office, they will call his parents."

"Okay, I won't be long," the monitor said, taking the boy into the building.

Eva knew the bus driver was always responsible for the kids on the bus, even if no one else cared. She sat back in her seat and thought about being home, hoping that by tomorrow, she'd feel better.

28
Night Hockey

Kenny gave Boris a night charter. He had to take the men's hockey team from R.I. College to play a game in Massachusetts.

Driving in the dark on 95 and 495, it took them almost an hour to get there. Boris had written directions and a map to follow. He took the correct exit and within minutes, he found the place. It was a large sports complex that was lit up in the night. He parked the bus and the young men were eager to unload their hockey equipment.

Boris liked the sport, so he went inside to watch the game. He was surprised to see girls skating on the ice, slamming into each other. They were dressed in full gear and were very athletic. They were fun to watch and they played with such emotion, he was sorry to see the game end.

It was cold inside the ice rink. He was glad he was wearing his heavy black coat. During intermission, he went to the snack bar for something hot to drink and bought a cup of coffee.

The college game started late. The young men from his bus played well and scored often. When the game was over, it was almost midnight.

Going back, it was raining and the street lights glared in the night. The return trip seemed faster with less traffic. When Boris dropped the team off at their dorm, the men were tired and sleepy.

JOHN FULCO

Pulling into Turner Yard, he didn't see a security guard. He gazed into the darkness and there wasn't anyone around. He carefully parked his bus and went to his car. It was the last car left in the lot.

When he returned home, his wife met him at the door in her pajamas.

"I thought you got lost," she said.

"They played late," he said.

"Well, at least it's Saturday, you can sleep in the morning.

The next day his wife, Mary, made pancakes and sausage for breakfast. She was a wonderful cook. Most of the time, her meals were better than what you'd get in a restaurant.

His mother told him once, "If you ever find a girl that can cook and is good in bed, you better marry her."

When he finished eating, he sat and read the morning paper. He was still thinking of starting his own business. There was an empty lot across the street with enough space to park buses. It was for sale and he thought about buying it.

29
Drug Test

Jack Miller had a busload of children. He was driving them to George West Elementary School. One of the boys had his hand up for a long time.

"What do you want?" the monitor asked him.

"Can we eat fish next Monday?" the boy asked.

"Why do you ask that?"

"Because it's Vegetarian Day," the boy said.

"It's Veterans Day, not Vegetarian Day," the monitor laughed.

"A veteran is someone who was in the army, like me. I'm an army veteran," Jack said.

"So I don't have to eat fish," the boy said, still confused.

"You can eat anything you want," the monitor said.

Jack stopped at the school and let the kids out, before returning to the yard. He dropped off the monitor and parked his bus, hurrying to the restroom.

He had to go, but two guys were waiting in line ahead of him. There were a couple of hundred drivers with only one restroom for men and one for women. Most of the time he held it until he was home, but his bladder was about to burst. No one was using the ladies' room, so he rushed in and locked the door behind him. He came out feeling relieved and rang his time card. Linda Stevens caught his attention.

"Jack, you have to go for a drug test," she said.

"A what?" He had no idea what she meant.

"Every month we pick several drivers for a drug test," she said. "It's done by random."

"Where do I have to go?"

"St. Joseph's Hospital on Broad Street," she said.

"I have to go now…"

"Yes, now. That's how it's done, without any notice. It's on the third floor." She gave him some medical papers that were clipped together for him to sign.

"Okay, I guess I have to go," he said. He didn't understand why they'd chosen him. Did they think he was on drugs or something?

He went to the hospital and met two other drivers. They were sitting in the waiting room. A woman dressed in white took his name and told him to have a drink of water from the cooler. He thought it was ironic: he had just emptied his bladder less than thirty minutes ago, and now he was supposed to pee again. He took a paper cup and started drinking.

"Is this your first test?" a driver asked him.

"Yes," Jack said.

"They have me do this every year," the driver said.

"And you have to do it?" Jack said.

"If you want to keep your job."

The same woman came and took the two other men, leaving Jack alone. He still had no urge, so he drank some more water. She came back twenty minutes later.

"Are you ready now?" she asked.

"No, because I went like a race horse less than an hour ago," Jack said.

"Well, you have to do it again," she said. "So drink lots of water."

"I am."

"Walk around. Move your arms and legs," she said. "I'll come back again."

He strolled up and down the long hallway a couple of times. He drank more water and still couldn't go.

The nurse checked back with him.

"Sorry," he said.

"Drink more water," she said.

"I drank a gallon."

"Try jumping up and down." She left again.

He drank even more water. He was there for more than an hour before he finally had the urge. She took him into the testing room and gave him a plastic cup to fill. He had to use a small enclosed toilet. The nurse stayed on the other side of the room listening to every move. He had no trouble going and felt embarrassed as he came out holding the cup of urine in his hand.

"You did it!" She took the cup and congratulated him. "Good for you," she said.

"How long does it take to get the results?" he asked.

"They have to send it to Massachusetts for testing. It takes a couple of days," she said. "Now you have to do a breathalyzer test."

"Anything for the company," he said.

That evening Jack went to Stony Brook. He had enough casino points for dinner. His wife Betty came with him and was expecting a nice meal. She liked going to the buffet for the salad bar. Jack always loaded his plate with food and made a pig of himself, because it was free.

After eating, they walked through the casino. It was packed again with gambling zombies, people who were half asleep with tired faces and bloodshot eyes. He gave his wife a hundred dollars to play the slots. She found a machine and right away, she won twenty bucks. He left her there and headed for the roulette tables.

Jack seemed to have more luck at roulette than any other game. He stood near a table watching the action for a time. Most of the numbers coming up were 2, 12, 21, 26, and 32. Every number had a two in it, giving him an idea. Why not play them all.

Someone left the table, leaving a spot open for him. He bought one hundred dollars worth of chips and covered every number with a two. Some squares he split with a chip between them, some he played straight up. Altogether, he had thirteen numbers covered. He lost a couple of times, then won several times in a row. For the next hour he was lucky and kept winning.

He switched to five-dollar chips. Betting heavy, he was ahead over a thousand dollars. The two's kept hitting and his winning chips were piling up. Everyone was watching him. Soon the floor boss came over to the table, along with another dealer. The new man spun the wheel, but Jack didn't bet. He watched as double zero came out and everyone lost.

He had been standing for almost two hours. His back was bothering him, so he sat down to have a drink, counting his chips. He was ahead more than he'd realized, almost three grand. It was the most money he had ever won.

"Cash me in," he said.

The dealer took his chips, stacking them into neat piles and counting them, exchanging them for black hundred dollar chips. Jack was all smiles and left a generous tip before going to the cashier, then he went to find his wife. She was still playing the quarter machines.

"How you doing, dear?" He could see her tray was full of coins.

"I'm winning," she said. "How'd you do, Jack?"

"I did good. I won a couple of hundred," he lied to her. If he told her the truth, she would have wanted to go on a cruise.

30
Turkey Day

Rossi and Laurie spent Thanksgiving Day at her brother's home. Danny owned a large two-family house in the town of North Kingston. He had a tree cutting and landscaping business. His two teenage children were active in school sports and his wife, Connie, was pregnant again. They gathered around the table in the dining room talking and eating turkey.

"This is nice," Rossi said to Laurie.

"My brother and his wife do this every year," she replied.

"Thank you for having us," Rossi said to her brother.

"'tis the season," he said.

After dinner, Laurie helped Connie clean up in the kitchen. They put everything in the dishwasher, then they all gathered around the table again and played board games.

Later in the day, the six of them went bicycle riding near a lake, where they stopped to rest. Danny had his camera and took pictures of everyone before they continued on down the road.

The next morning at Rossi's house, he was up early. He pulled the scale out from under the bed, weighing himself, and wasn't happy with the results. He thought about going on a diet. He went to the kitchen and opened a can of cat food. Tommy Boy came flying into the room and smelled the dish of chicken on the floor. He turned up his nose and walked away.

"What? You don't want it," he said. "Well, you're not getting anything else."

He took his vitamins with a glass of water and went outside to exercise. First, twenty pushups, then some sit-ups and a couple of minutes with the jump rope, before going jogging.

It was still early and the streets were empty. He needed to run hard, because he ate too much turkey over the holiday. As he moved along the sidewalk, pumping his legs up and down, he was thinking of Laurie. He promised to take her someplace for the weekend, but he didn't know where. When he was young and single, he went to New Hampshire, so he thought about going there. It should be nice this time of the year. Something in the road caught his attention. He bent down and picked it up. It was a small sterling cross. He held it in his hand and continued to run.

The sun was coming up and the sky turned bright blue. The weather report was for a good weekend; he hoped it was right. Sweating profusely, he cut across the street in front of Mount Pleasant High School and jogged back home. Laurie was just getting out of bed when he came in the house.

"Good morning," he said cheerfully.

"You're up early," she said.

"I was thinking about going to New Hampshire."

"New Hampshire?" She seemed surprised.

"Have you ever been there?" he asked her.

"No, never."

"I went there once," he said. "The White Mountains are beautiful, with lakes and little towns."

"I'll have to think about it," she said.

"I found this in the street." He gave her the silver cross. "Maybe you can use it."

"Thanks, Ross," she said, examining it. "It's lovely. I can wear it around my neck."

"Well, we have to get ready," he said. "I'm going to shower and shave."

31
Up North

Rossi dressed and packed a duffle bag with a change of underwear, his toothbrush, and some other things. He put down fresh litter for the cat and left an extra bowl of dry food and plenty of water.

Laurie was painting her toenails with red polish. She started experimenting with makeup on her face, sometimes using too much. She checked her belly. The doctor said she was pregnant, but she still wasn't showing.

"Are you really going to New Hampshire?"

"Of course," he said.

"Okay, I'll get ready." She didn't believe him at first.

"Do you need anything from your place?" he asked.

"No," she said.

"We're going to be gone for a couple of days. You might need a change of clothes."

"Are you taking anything?" she asked.

"Just some underwear."

"Well, I think I'm all set."

"What about your toothbrush?" he asked.

"I can use my finger," she said and laughed.

"Okay then, let's go," he said, picking up his bag. "If you need anything, I'll buy it."

They stopped at a mini-mart that had gas. Rossi filled the tank with fuel and checked the oil stick. Laurie went into the store and came back with an orange soda and a pack of cigarettes, then they settled into the car.

"Ready?" he asked.

"Let's go," she said.

They traveled through Boston and over a high bridge. Rossi knew the way. He just followed the signs until they came to Route 16. As they went along, Laurie listened to country music on the radio. It was a long ride from Rhode Island to New Hampshire. Passing by thick green woods, Rossi could feel a change in the air and could smell the pine trees. It was really refreshing. Something was in the road ahead of them and the traffic was slowing. It was a toll booth.

"I've never seen a toll road." Laurie was amused.

"Yeah, you have to pay," he said.

"I don't believe it," she said.

"It's only fifty cents," he said, throwing two quarters into the coin basket.

"That's terrible," she said.

"I know, but it's their road and if you want to get there, you have to pay," he said.

Sometime later, they turned off the road and came to a large lake. The water was murky gray with fishing boats floating along the surface. There were a few houses near the lake with people working in the yards.

"It's a big lake," Laurie said.

"It's called Lake Winnipesaukee."

"The air seems different," she said, taking a deep breath.

"There's no pollution around here."

They came to Weirs Beach, where there was a boardwalk and a string of concession stands. After finding a place to park, they left the car to stretch their legs.

"There must be a lot of fish in this water," she said.

"I bet there is," he said.

The waves were lapping gently along the shore and a few mallard ducks swam nearby. A tourist boat left the dock and leisurely moved away into deeper water.

"It's nice, isn't it?" he said.

"I could get used to this," she said.

"It's like coming to another world," he said.

Most of the stands were closed as they strolled down the boardwalk. They came to a small restaurant that was open.

"I'm getting hungry," he said. "Let's get something to eat." He led her inside to a table. Breakfast was still being served.

There was a wonderful view of the lake from where they were sitting. They both had eggs with home fries, toast, and coffee. Rossi didn't talk much until he had finished eating, then he told her about the time he came here when he was younger.

"Really, did you come alone?" she asked.

"No, a friend came with me, a buddy."

"I hope you had a different car." She laughed.

"What are you thinking, of course I had another car, that was years ago."

After, they went walking along the boardwalk.

"Look, they're open," she said, pulling him into a gift shop.

"Laurie, do you see anything you like?"

"I'm just looking," she said.

"How about this?!" He showed her a shirt with a big red tongue on it.

"Yikes!" she said.

"I like this one," she said, holding up a black tee shirt with the words "New Hampshire."

"I'm buying it for you," he said.

On the way back to the car, they found an empty bench overlooking the water. They sat there for awhile and she smoked a cigarette. He had some good cigars on him so he unwrapped one and lit it.

"Where did you get that thing?" She looked at him in disbelief.

"I bought it the other day," he said.

"I didn't know you smoked cigars."

"Do you mind?"

"No, go ahead."

"It's my secret," he said.

"What is?" she asked.

"When I want to feel like a millionaire, I just smoke a good cigar or drink some expensive wine."

"You're weird," she said.

They drove north again and went through the small town of Meredith, eventually coming back to Route 16. Passing Oseepee Lake, they kept going until they came to Conway. A festival was being held with crowds of people along the street. The traffic was slow. A high school band was marching down the middle of the street. Town banners hung from poles and there was a flea market.

The White Mountains loomed before them. Rossi drove further, coming to North Conway, where there were more restaurants and motels. He pulled into a gas station.

"Is everything all right?" Laurie asked him.

"Just need gas," he said, getting out. He pumped fuel into the tank and noticed a soda machine. "Do you want another soda, Laurie?"

"No thanks," she said.

He paid the attendant and drove up the road, coming to a large park that was next to a railroad station. They stopped there and rested in the car. The mountain range completely surrounded them. There was a movie theater across the street and a five-and-dime store on the corner.

"They have everything here." Laurie seemed surprised.

"Even the latest movies," Rossi said.

"Let's go over there," Laurie said, pointing to a building on the corner. "I'd like to see what they have in the store." Rossi followed her into the five-and-dime. They had several racks of tee shirts and lots of souvenirs. She examined just about every knick-knack in the place, but couldn't make up her mind on what to buy. She had a sweet tooth and couldn't resist the large assortment of penny candy. She bought some black licorice and chewed a stick after leaving the store.

There was a miniature golf course that looked interesting.

"Let's play," she said.

"The winner gets a massage tonight," Rossi said.

"What kind of massage?" She giggled.

"A real hot one." He winked at her.

She held the golf club in her hands and hit the ball. It bounced off a rock in the wrong direction. He took his turn. His ball went straight into the hole.

"What a lucky shot," she said.

"Looks like I'm going to get a massage tonight." He smiled.

They played the course. Laurie had fun, but she didn't play

well. She kept hitting the ball too hard.

"I need practice," she said.

He tried to help her with her swing, but she was a terrible shot. "We need to get a motel room later," he said.

There was a card and gift shop across the street.

"Let's go see what they have," she said, after they finished.

"Why not, maybe I'll find a vibrator for a massage," he laughed.

"You don't need one," she said, entering the shop.

They had greeting cards, candies, paperback books, and boxes of puzzles. She liked to do puzzles. She found one with five hundred pieces and Rossi bought it for her.

There were more than a dozen motels with vacancy signs. They decided on one that was rated triple A and went inside the room with their things, a duffle bag, her new puzzle, and a bag of candy. She sat on the bed while he checked out the bathroom. The place was clean with new furniture and a large screen TV.

"I like this bed," she said. "It's nice and firm."

"I have something nice and firm too," he said, lying on the bed next to her.

"You do," she said, jumping on him. "Prove it..."

Their clothes came off in a minute, then they kissed. He held her nude body in his arms, rolling on top of her. He liked having sex with her; she was so loving and irresistible.

He lay there afterwards, watching television. He was tired from the long drive and soon fell asleep. She was wide awake and decided to get dressed and go somewhere. Leaving on the television, she left the room.

Sometime later, Rossi woke up. The space next to him in bed was empty. On the table were an open bottle of vodka and a carton

PASSING THROUGH PROVIDENCE

of orange juice. He could hear water running in the bathroom.

"Are you taking a shower?" he asked, getting no answer. He knocked on the bathroom door. "Hello."

"I'm almost finished," she said. "Did you have a nice nap?"

"Yes, I was tired."

A few minutes later, she appeared wearing only her bra and panties.

"Where'd you get the vodka?" he asked.

"I went to the liquor store while you were sleeping. I felt like getting a little crazy, so I bought something to drink. What about you, Ross?"

"I guess I'm going crazy too," he said, picking up the bottle. He took a long drink.

"Pour me another one," she said.

"You can't have any more, because you're pregnant."

"Oh, all right, then I'll just have some juice."

He started flipping the channels on the television. "Well, look at this," he said. It was a movie about Las Vegas showgirls who were dancing around half naked. "Wow, look at those girls move," he said.

"You know, I've got moves too." She stood up dancing, swinging her hips in front of him. "How's that?" she said.

"More, more," he begged her. He pulled out his harmonica and started playing. She liked the sounds and moved her body with the music. She took off her top, twirling it over her head. She was just wearing panties. "Shake it!" he shouted. He kept playing a tune and was getting excited. She turned her back on him, wiggling her behind in his face before sitting in his lap and kissing his neck. He dropped the harmonica to the floor and put his arms around her, then they fell into bed again.

Later, Rossi was lying there exhausted with a big smile on his face. She was out cold and snoring. He didn't need to sleep, so he went into the bathroom and took a long shower. When he was done, he got dressed and picked up a wet face cloth, dropping it over her face. She sat up and moaned.

"Where am I?" she said, opening her eyes.

"With me, remember?"

"How could I forget?" she said.

"I want to go eat," he said.

"Right now?"

"As soon as you're ready," he said.

"Give me five minutes," she said.

"I can wait," he said.

It was nighttime now and the city lights were glowing. They left the car in the center of town and went for a walk, coming to a restaurant that had the dinner menu posted next to the door. Laurie read it and didn't see anything she wanted. The night air was cool as they continued along the way. She was awake now and felt better. There was a hotel that had a buffet dinner with beef stroganoff.

"What do you think, Ross?"

"Let's try it," he said. "I'm so hungry, I could eat a moose."

"Really," she said, giggling.

The dining room was busy with several couples eating. The food smelled wonderful. He paid the cashier eighteen dollars for the two of them. Along with the beef stroganoff, there was ham, chicken, salad, and dessert. The meal was well worth the price. They sat at a table with their plates full and ate.

"This is delicious," Laurie said.

"Very good," Rossi agreed between mouthfuls. "I'm going

back for seconds."

The next morning, he peeked out the window of the motel and saw the ground covered with snow. Excited, he dressed and sneaked outside, scooping up a handful of the white flakes. He took something from his pocket that he had gotten for Laurie last week. He pushed it carefully into the snowball and went back inside.

"Hello, Laurie, hello."

She sat up in bed with sleepy eyes.

"Look what I have for you." He presented it to her. "Da-dah," he said.

"A snowball…are you crazy?!" She held it in her hands. "Where'd you get this?"

"Outside, it snowed last night."

"I should throw it at you for waking me up," she said.

"You're holding something very special."

"I am…." she said, confused.

"Inside the snowball," he said.

"I hope it doesn't bite." She poked her fingers through it.

"No, but I might," he said.

She felt something and pulled it out. Her face lit up when she saw what it was: a diamond ring.

32
Driving Test

Lenny Harris and his trainees loaded onto a bus for Quonset Point. It was early in the morning and a trainee drove. They were going to the testing sight for their driver's license. Lenny was like a football coach trying to encourage them.

"This is the time you've been waiting for," he said. "You had the training, now you know what to do."

"What if I don't pass?" Ida, the black girl, said.

"You have to think positive," Lenny said. "I know you are all going to pass. Remember, the bus company pays the fee today. If you fail, it will cost you twenty-five dollars the next time."

They rode from the city into North Kingstown, coming to Quonset Point. It used to be a naval base where thousands of military personnel were stationed. Now, it was being used for private industry and some of the Quonset huts were for commercial storage.

They followed a narrow road through the base until they came to an area the size of a football field. It was covered with asphalt and was the testing area. There were no buildings around, only a lone portable toilet. A dozen orange cones were laid out in different locations. A man was waiting in his car; he was the state examiner.

Everyone stepped out of the bus except Ida. Only one driver

at a time could take the test. Everyone else had to wait their turn. The man left his car and came on the bus, giving her instructions.

There were three parts to the test. Ida passed the first two parts, the pre-trip and the horizontal parking. The last part was the road test, where you had to drive off base.

The man told her what streets to follow through town and where to turn. When they came to a set of railroad tracks, she stopped the bus and turned on the orange blinking lights and opened the door. "I look both ways and listen for a train," she said. "When I see nothing, I go." She stepped on the accelerator and closed the door.

"You're supposed to close the door before you leave," the inspector told her.

"I won't forget next time," she said.

All the trainees huddled together waiting for the bus to come back, so they could take their turn. It was a wide open area with no shelter, and the wind was freezing.

"Man, it's cold," Lenny said, rubbing his hands. He wished he could sit on the bus and get warm, but that was not allowed during testing. He was thinking about quitting the job and buying a boat to catch fish. He was getting tired of driving every day, but he needed to pay for his car first. Maybe one more bank job, he thought.

"How long are we gonna be here?" someone said

"As long as it takes," Lenny said.

"Maybe all morning?" someone else moaned.

It was around one o'clock in the afternoon before the last trainee finished. Everyone was glad to get back on the bus where it was warm.

"Congratulations! Everyone passed," Lenny said to them.

"You're all bus drivers. Now let's get something hot to drink before I freeze to death."

For the next few days, Lenny had no training classes scheduled. He was given some time off, so he left for Atlantic City in his Caddy. He took Carmella with him and was going to party. He stashed some money in the trunk of his car and felt rich with the roll of bills in his pocket.

It was a long ride to New Jersey. When he came to the beach, he pulled into the casino garage. He helped Carmella from the car with her suitcase, then they went inside the hotel lobby. He had reservations and was given a room on the eighth floor. There was a king-size bed with a mirrored ceiling over it and a large Jacuzzi bathtub in the corner, along with a breathtaking view of the ocean from the window.

"I could stay here forever," Carmella said, giving him a big kiss as they fell into bed.

33
A Strange Lady

The temperature in the afternoon was eighteen degrees, and it felt like zero with the wind chill. Eva Gomez was taking the kids home in her bus. She had the heat on high, but it still felt cold. Driving along the streets, she passed stores and homes that were decorated with Christmas lights throughout the city. Everyone was getting ready for the holidays.

Each year, the Turner Company awarded the best drivers with an extra week's pay. She received hers and was thinking about doing some shopping.

"Eighty to Kenny," someone said over the two-way. "This is an emergency!"

"Go ahead," Kenny answered.

"I was going down Route 95 and someone shot out one of my windows."

"Is everyone all right?"

"Everyone is okay," the driver said. "I only have two kids left, then I'm coming back to the yard.

"Ten-four," Kenny said, "I'm calling the police right now."

More broken windows, Eva was thinking. She was waiting for a red light at an intersection. An old man walking in the street knocked on the bus door.

"What do you want?" she said. He pointed at the door. "Sorry,

I can't open it for strangers."

"But I need a ride into town," he said.

"This is a school bus. You have to catch the city bus," Eva told him, driving away. "Stupid old man," she said. She had three kids left. She went another block, letting them go, then returned to the yard.

She always checked inside the bus. A few drivers were fired for leaving sleeping children on the bus. She didn't need that to happen to her. She took her time sweeping the floor. She was getting paid by the hour anyway and the extra minutes added up to a bigger paycheck. She sat for awhile and read a newspaper from yesterday, turning the pages. The paper was loaded with sales; every store had an ad. She was hoping to find something for her family. She saw a picture of a black man wanted for robbery, but she couldn't recognize his face because he wore dark glasses and a black baseball cap.

When she'd finished, she went home and cooked supper for her children. She always made sure they had a good meal and did their homework before playing. Her husband was at work and would be home late. While washing dishes, she heard a knock on the door. Looking through the window, she saw a strange woman. She was Hispanic and had bleached blond hair. She opened the door.

"Hello. Does Luis live here?" she asked.

"Yes," Eva said.

"Are you his wife?"

"Yes. Can I help you?"

"My name is Blanca Martinez. I need to talk with you about your husband."

"Talk about what?" Eva asked. The woman was young, no more than twenty years old.

"I'm pregnant. I'm sorry to tell you this, but Luis is the father.

He didn't tell me he was married."

"Eva felt her blood pressure rising. "Come in," she said. They went into the kitchen and sat at the table.

"I didn't know he was married. I'm sorry," the woman said again.

"You know, he has three kids." Eva was trying to remain calm.

"He has three kids with you?"

"Yes."

"I'm sorry, I didn't know."

"That no good bastard!" Eva shouted in anger.

Her son, who was in the other room, came into the kitchen.

"Is something wrong, Mom?"

"This is private. Go and play," she told him and gave the woman a cup of coffee.

"I thought he was going to marry me," the young lady said. "He was giving me a ride home. And I let him come into my apartment."

"So, what are you going to do about the baby?" Eva asked her.

"I'm having an abortion right away."

"You don't want the baby?"

"No, not now. I'm going back to Columbia to live." After having coffee, the young woman told Eva how sorry she was again and left the house.

Eva couldn't hold back the tears any longer and started crying. She'd thought her husband was cheating on her; now she knew for sure. Her son peeked in the kitchen and saw her wiping her face.

"What's wrong, Mom?"

"There's nothing wrong," she said.

"Who was that lady?" he asked.

"You don't need to know," she said. "I'm all right now. Go play."

She was so upset, she couldn't sleep that night. When Luis came home, she waited until he was in the bedroom before confronting him. She told him what had happened.

"I don't know this lady," he told her.

"You lying bastard!" She slapped him across the face. "You are not sleeping here."

"Stop this!" he said, backing away from her.

"You liar," she cried.

"I don't know her." He could see the rage in her face. He tried talking with her, but it was useless.

"You bastard, get the hell away from me!"

He had to leave and went downstairs. He sat in the living room and hoped everything would be all right tomorrow. He watched TV and fell asleep on the couch. When morning came, he tried to talk with her again, begging her forgiveness.

"You can go to hell!" she told him.

34
Deadly Roulette

Jack Miller returned to Stony Brook again. The casino was swarming with people like bees in the hive. He was feeling lucky and wanted to play blackjack, but every seat was taken. He waited for awhile, then he went over to watch the roulette players. There was a woman betting twenty-five dollar chips on each spin of the wheel. She put down several chips each time and was losing a bundle. She couldn't catch a number.

Jack had to play; he just couldn't stand there any longer. He noticed even numbers were coming up, so he bet even and won. He liked to go with the flow. He raised his bets and won sixty dollars. He needed to win a lot more, but how? he wondered. He was still watching the woman who was losing all her money. The stack of chips in front of her was gone. She turned away with her eyes full of tears and fled.

Jack was feeling hopeless again. He was winning a small amount, not the thousands he needed. Everyone around him was losing. His confidence was fading fast. He took his chips and went for a walk around the casino and thought about going home. If he could just make a big hit.

He stopped at the five-dollar slot machines and decided to play, buying a hundred dollars in coins from the change girl. Maybe he could hit a big jackpot. He put two coins in the slot and pulled the handle and the reels spun. He didn't win, so he tried again. He made a couple of small hits, enough to keep playing for twenty minutes, but it was useless.

The hundred was gone in no time. He knew he had to leave, and went outside to get some air and saw a crowd of people gathered around in the parking lot. A red rescue truck pulled up. A woman was lying on the ground.

"She's dead," a man said.

Jack moved closer for a better look. It was the woman who was playing roulette. Her head was in a pool of blood. She'd shot herself.

I need to get away from here, Jack thought, this is madness. He found his car and was never coming back.

He turned on the radio and tried listening to some music as he drove. He thought about the dead woman and about ending it all. He had a large life insurance policy and his wife would get the money. He drove faster, going from 50 to 100 mph in no time. The wind was whistling by the windows, when he heard a voice—bankruptcy, it said. You can claim bankruptcy and get rid of all your bills. It was a woman's voice, a voice from the dead…or was it a radio commercial? He thought about it for a moment, then slowed the car down. Bankruptcy seemed like a good idea.

He passed some cows and a barn, then he slowed down. He saw a large flock of birds in a field and stopped to get a better look. They were big birds, and then he realized they were wild turkeys. He lit a cigarette and continued home.

The next morning, he finished his bus run and had a charter for an elementary school. He parked in front of the school and waited. When he had a chance, he was going to call a lawyer about claiming bankruptcy. He needed to have more information before telling his wife. He really didn't want to say anything to her; he dreaded the moment.

A teacher came from the school with a trail of minority kids following him.

"We're going to the Marriot Hotel," the teacher told Jack.

Each child came on the bus carrying a bag with a swimsuit and towel. The teacher sat in front.

"That's a nice place," Jack said, amused.

"We're going swimming," the teacher said. "The pool is always warm and I get to sit in the hot tub."

"The city pays for all this?" Jack said.

"Well, I sure don't," the teacher said. Some of the kids were fooling around. He turned and yelled at them. "If you want to go swimming, you had better be quiet."

The hotel wasn't far. After a short ride, Jack dropped them off at the main entrance.

"See you back here in a couple of hours," the teacher said.

Up the road, there was a large plaza with a donut shop. Jack went there and parked the bus where it was safe. He went inside the place for a coffee and a muffin.

After he was served, he took a seat near the window, then he saw a guy pull up in a mail jeep. When the guy came in for coffee, Jack waved him over to his table. "Sit down and take a rest," he said. "I'm a retired mailman. See, I'm still wearing my postal sweater."

"What city did you work in?" the carrier asked.

"I was in Johnston the last eight years," Jack said. "My back was killing me and they had early retirement, so I took it."

"I have a long way to go before I can retire," the carrier said.

"I hated the winters with all the snow and ice," Jack said.

"I know what you mean," the carrier said. "Did you ever have any problems with supervisors?"

"Yeah, they were always watching me. One day they got mad because I went to the bathroom, twice," Jack said, laughing.

"They don't even like it when I use my sick days," said the carrier, taking a sip of his coffee.

"Yeah, you take a sick day and they crucify you for it," Jack said. "And you know why postage stamps keep going up?"

"I think I know why," the guy said.

"Too many chiefs and not enough Indians." Jack could shoot the breeze about the post office all day long.

After awhile, the guy glanced at his watch. "Well, my break is over. Nice talking with you."

"Watch out for those supervisors," Jack said. "They'll have you running your route like a race horse." When he finished his coffee, he drove the bus back to the hotel and picked up the kids.

35
Fired

Boris bought a bus from a tour company. It wasn't a big bus, but it was large enough to hold thirty people. It ran good and had new tires. He signed a contract with them, so he could use their garage for any repairs. He had to change the name on the side of the bus and put his phone number on it. He used it for a few charters and parked it in his driveway.

Once he took a load of teachers from Johnson & Wales College to Green Airport in Warwick. He made a hundred bucks for the trip and they gave him a ten-dollar tip.

"See you when we get back," a teacher told him.

"Have a nice time," Boris said, putting the money in his pocket.

The next day, he was playing Ping-Pong in the drivers' lounge. No one could beat him.

"I'm the champion," he boasted, then Linda Stevens called him into her office. He went in and took a seat, expecting bad news.

"A customer called to thank us for the trip they had to Mystic Sea Port. Did you take them on a charter?" she asked him.

"It wasn't me, maybe someone else used the bus," he said.

"But it was you. They gave your bus number and said it was a bald-headed guy. Anyway, we checked the fuel list and found out that you used twice as much fuel over the last month."

"It wasn't me," he lied again.

"You can't drive our bus and burn our fuel anytime you feel like it. As of now, you're fired and don't come back for your paycheck."

Boris knew this day was coming, but he didn't really care. Now he was ready to start his own company.

36
To See a Doctor

In December, Laurie packed up her belongings and moved into Rossi's house. With a baby coming, she needed to save money. She was four-months pregnant and determined to go through with it. She filed for divorce from her husband. That part of her life was over and she wanted to forget it.

Rossi was a happy guy since she was living with him; having female company was like heaven to him. He was keeping busy by doing extra charters. One day he came home from the store with a container of pitted dates.

"Are those olives?" Laurie asked him.

"No, silly," he laughed. "Dates."

"Dates, I never had any. Are they good?"

"After I stuff them, you can try some. I make them every year at Christmastime." He put everything on the table, then opened a bag of walnut meats and poured some powdered sugar into a bowl. "This is how you do it." He put some chunks of nuts inside the pitted dates and rolled them in sugar. In ten minutes time, he made three different kinds. "Here, try one," he said.

She put it in her mouth. "Hmm, these are good," she said, chewing. "Better than candy." She tried a couple more. She liked the ones filled with chunky peanut butter and rolled in brown sugar the most.

"How did you learn to make them?" she asked.

"From my grandmother."

The next morning when Laurie sat on the side of the bed, she noticed her ankles were swollen. She didn't know why. She was eating a normal diet and only gained about five pounds. As soon as Rossi was awake, she showed him her feet. He suggested she see a doctor soon.

"And I think you better stay home this morning," he said.

"I'll try to get an appointment," she said.

Rossi went to work on a cold cloudy day and was dressed in a warm winter coat with corduroy pants, wearing his baseball cap. He was doing his first run without a monitor, driving and watching the kids. It was the last day of the week and the kids were more trouble than ever. Most of the middle school girls were wearing black lipstick and smelled of perfume. JoVon was sitting quietly by himself, his face hidden with a hooded sweatshirt. The Thomas twins kept poking each other and having a shouting match.

Rossi slowed the bus down. "I'm going to report you to the principal," he said. The boys stopped and played cool. Satisfied, he continued to the next street and loaded more kids before heading for the school.

There was a loud disturbance—the twins were bickering again. Rossi was tired of them. He called the dispatcher and reported them.

JoVon jumped from his seat and pulled the two boys apart. "Chill out, man," he said. His hood slipped off and everyone could see his shiny bald head. He looked like a black Mr. Clean. He was much bigger and stronger than anyone else. No one said a word for the rest of the way.

PASSING THROUGH PROVIDENCE

The principal was waiting on the street when they arrived and escorted the twins to his office. Rossi was glad to get rid of them. He didn't know what their problem was, he just wished they'd act better.

His tenant, Sadie Smith, was having her birthday today, and he promised to take her out to dinner. He hoped Laurie would feel like going along. He did his other run, taking the elementary kids to school, then returned to the bus yard.

When he went home, Laurie told him she had a doctor's appointment.

"They had some cancellations, so they said I could come in this morning."

"That's good," he said. "I'll just be a second." He had to use the bathroom. He was peeing more than ever. Maybe it was an age thing.

Twenty minutes later, he dropped her off at the medical building, waiting until she was inside before leaving. He felt like having a coffee. Hundreds of donut shops were located in Providence, so finding one was easy.

Laurie gave her name to the receptionist and took a seat in the waiting room. Only a few people were there. She hoped she wouldn't be long. There were some magazines on the counter. She picked up one and started to read.

After awhile, someone called her name and she was directed to a room. A nurse put her on a scale and weighed her, then took her blood pressure. The doctor came and introduced himself. He bent down to examine her ankles and her legs. "It looks like you have toxemia," he said. "Let me listen to your heart." He took his stethoscope and placed it on her chest and kept moving it around.

"Anything wrong?" Laurie asked.

"No, just making sure," he said. "I want you to stay off your feet for the next couple of days. Keep them elevated on a pillow."

"But I have to work, I'm a bus monitor," she said.

"Well, stay home a day or two, then maybe you can go back to work. For now, you need to keep off your feet as much as possible, okay?"

She had to give some blood for the lab to analyze before leaving.

"Where'd you go?" she asked Rossi when he picked her up.

"To get a donut and some coffee."

"And you didn't get me a donut?"

"Maybe next time."

"Cheapskate!"

"Well, I'm buying dinner."

"I hope so, I'm hungry."

Instead of taking Sadie Smith to a restaurant for dinner, Rossi ordered Chinese food to go and took it home. He bought a birthday cake too and the three of them had a good time.

37
To Trash a Bus

Saturday morning Dwayne Thomas was up early and was in a bad mood. During the week he had to find his own way to school, because the principal suspended him from Rossi's bus. He and his brother were living with their grandfather for the past year. Their mother's whereabouts were unknown.

A gun was hidden in the house and Dwayne knew where it was located. While everyone was sleeping, he took the weapon and headed downtown. He went to the wall in Providence where runaways and school kids hung out. The wall was only knee-high and made of concrete and no one was there except an old homeless man begging for money.

Dwayne knew where a café was around the corner. He went there for a cup of cocoa and to pass the time. He sat at the counter and didn't see anyone he knew. A guy sitting next to him finished his breakfast, leaving a dollar tip. The waitress was busy, so Dwayne grabbed the buck and hurried outside. He ran into a prostitute who was standing on the sidewalk looking for an early score.

"Any freebees today?" he asked her.

"Get lost, junior," she grumbled.

He saw two boys sitting on the wall. They were wearing baggy pants and talking.

"Hey Rafael, what's up, man," Dwayne said.

"Dwayne, where you been hanging?"

"School, man. So, what's happening?"

"We're just waiting for Benny and his car. Then we're going cruising," Rafael said.

"I'm packing a rod, man," Dwayne said.

"No way." Rafael didn't believe him.

"Look." Dwayne pulled the gun halfway out of his coat pocket.

"Wow, is it loaded?"

"Yeah, I'm gonna have some fun," Dwayne said.

"Like what, hold up a bank?"

"No way, man, I'm just having a little target practice."

"What target?"

"A yellow bus, man, you know, a school bus. You wanna come?"

"Sure, what the hell," Rafael said.

His friend Benny came with his car and gave them a ride. They rode across town and were dropped off a block from Turner Yard. They walked along the road to a wire fence and climbed over it. They didn't see anyone as they hid in the shadows.

"Why are we trashing this bus?" asked Rafael.

"Because, the driver's a rat. Follow me," Dwayne said, darting through the rows of buses. He was searching for number nineteen.

"Here it is," he said, pushing the door open and sneaking inside. Catching his breath, he sat in the driver's seat, taking a pack of cigarettes from his pocket. "Rafael, you wanna light up?"

"Cool, man."

They sat there for awhile smoking and talking.

After gaining more confidence, Dwayne said, "Let's do it, man," pulling the gun from his pocket. Suddenly they heard something and ducked down from sight. A bus moved quickly between the rows and disappeared.

They waited until it was quiet again, then Rafael found the fire extinguisher and pulled the pin. He sprayed the seats with white foam and made a mess. Dwayne held the gun and pulled the trigger, shooting out the front windshield and a couple of the side windows.

Pedro, the security guard, was making his routine rounds in the yard when he heard gun shots. He called the police on his cell phone.

The two boys saw him coming and ran toward the fence. A police car came within minutes and chased them down the road. The boys separated and went their own way.

Dwayne ran across the highway overpass. Coming to the other side, he leaped over the rail without thinking, falling a long way down. He landed on some rocks, hurting his leg and knocking himself unconscious.

38
A Tragedy

Lenny Harris went into Smithy's Diner. He was hungry and wanted some wieners. They came in small buns and were a treat to eat. He ordered three.

"With the works?" the counter man asked.

"The works and extra onions." Just the smell of them made his mouth water.

The man smothered the wieners with meat sauce and everything, then he wrapped them in wax paper.

Lenny went outside and sat in his Caddy and ate them. He was staying at Carmella's place now, getting some loving. He paid her bills, bought her some new clothes, and took her dancing. Sweet talking her was easy.

After lunch, he returned to Turner Yard to get his bus. He needed a couple of thousand dollars to pay off the loan on his car and had to do another bank job. Deep down inside him he knew it was wrong, but he needed his car.

Last week he cased a small bank in North Providence and was going there now. It was located at the top of a hill in a strip mall. He drove by with the bus and didn't see a security guard on duty.

He parked the bus on a side street across from a boarded up mill. No houses were around except for an old vacant building. Yesterday, he hid a bicycle there. He pulled it out and rode up the hill.

PASSING THROUGH PROVIDENCE

Halfway there, he started getting indigestion from the wieners. Why did he have those extra onions? He cursed himself for the acid in his gut. Stopping to rest, he pulled out a pack of peppermint gum from his pocket and tried chewing two sticks, swallowing the salvia. In a couple of minutes, he felt better.

He continued along until reaching the top of the hill. After he caught his breath, he gazed through the shaded glass window and saw that the bank was empty. Wearing his black baseball cap and sunglasses, he walked through the door and headed for the teller and gave her the note. She read it and turned white. Her co-worker was too busy talking on her cell phone.

"What are you waiting for?" Lenny showed her a gun.

Her eyes grew wide when she saw the weapon. Immediately, she started stacking the counter with bills. Within seconds, the money was in his coat pockets. He blew her a kiss and left.

He flew down the hill on the bike, turning into the street where he left the bus. He ditched the bike in some bushes and threw the gun into a sewer drain. Seeing no one around, he started the bus and drove away. He could hear police sirens in the distance.

"A piece of cake," he said to himself.

Carrying the money made him nervous, so he made a quick trip to Carmella's house to switch jackets. It took extra time getting there, but he felt better doing it. She wasn't home and wouldn't know anything.

Now he was running late, but he'd accomplished what he had to do. While driving his bus to the School for the Deaf, he thought about the money. He was going to pay his car loan first, then buy a fishing boat with the rest.

He was getting closer to the school when a Hispanic woman, carrying a baby, ran into the street and waved him down. She sounded hysterical. "My house is on fire! Help me," she pleaded. "My two girls are in the house!"

He could see black smoke coming from the roof. He reported the fire to the dispatcher first, then he rushed over to the front entrance of the house. Thick smoke blew in his face as he went into the hallway. He searched through a couple of rooms and his eyes started to burn. He thought he heard a girl crying.

The smoke was getting bad, so he dropped down, crawling into the next room where he found her hiding in a closet. He picked her up running through the smoke. He went out the front door and laid her down on the ground.

"Oh my God!" the mother cried. "My other girl is still in there!"

Lenny rushed through the hallway and crawled as far as he could before the intense heat stopped him. He started to leave when he saw a figure lying in the corner of a room. He moved closer to the body and touched her, but there was no response.

The flames were getting closer and he had to leave. He started to turn and the fire exploded in his face, blinding him. Panic-stricken, he tried to stand and fell backwards. A large wooden beam came loose and landed on him, pinning him to the floor.

The firemen came in minutes, but it was too late for Lenny and the girl.

39
The Funeral

Lenny's funeral was held the week before Christmas. It lasted for hours and everyone there was feeling sad. Turner Company provided two buses for the occasion. Jack Miller drove one of them, carrying drivers and monitors.

The local newspaper wrote an extensive story about how Lenny had saved a little girl's life. There were dozens of flowers around his casket. A minister prayed, then the mayor of Providence gave a long speech about how Lenny died a hero.

Carmella was there too, wiping her tears with a handkerchief. She was crying, but she wasn't telling anyone about the money she found inside Lenny's jacket. She just kept wiping the tears from her eyes.

Rudy Smith was there, dressed in a brown suit and tie. Someone else confessed to the crime and he was released.

Carmella was talking with Jack and Rossi.

"I thought he was in jail," she said.

"Who was in jail?" Rossi asked her.

"Him," she gestured. "Lenny's friend, Rudy Smith."

"I have to talk with him," Rossi said. He remembered reading about him in the paper, but that wasn't his business. He just wanted to see if Sadie Smith was his mother. He went over and introduced himself.

"Hi, I'm a bus driver for Turner yard. I'm just trying to find out if you know a lady called Sadie Smith?"

Rudy smiled when he heard the name. "The only Sadie I know is my mother."

"She's renting an apartment from me. I'll give you the address."

Rossi found a piece of paper in his pocket and wrote down the number and street.

"I hope you see her soon," he said.

"I will, I promise," Rudy said. "I had some problems for awhile and I was messed up on drugs, and I just lost track of her. Thanks, man."

After the funeral, Jack drove the bus with everyone back to Turner Yard, then he went home.

"How'd it go?" Betty said.

"I hate funerals. I hope I never go to another one," Jack said.

In the morning, he arrived at the lawyer's office on time and sat in a leather chair that smelled new. While he waited in the office, he wondered if he was doing the right thing.

A young woman came in from another room and introduced herself as the attorney. He was expecting someone older.

"Hello, I'm Jill Green. Can I help you?"

"I think I have to file for bankruptcy," Jack said. "I have too many bills."

"I see," she said, "so you're having trouble with the payments?"

"That's right." He told her about the thousands he owed on his credit cards.

She wrote down all the information and his address. She explained to him about chapter seven, the process they would have to go through, and about going to court. She also made a list of his credit cards and the amount he owed on each of them.

"My fee is five hundred dollars, payable in the first two weeks," she said.

"No problem," Jack said. He opened his wallet and gave her two hundred dollars for a deposit.

"Okay," she said. "Now you can't use your credit cards anymore, understand?"

"I understand," he said.

"If you do, it could mean complications," she said.

"I won't use them."

"It'll probably be several weeks before we go to court," she said. "You will be hearing from me."

"Thank you," he said, leaving. He thought she was very pleasant and very young, but age didn't matter if she could get rid of his bills.

He went home feeling better. Now he had to face his wife. She sat in the living room reading a book.

"Hi, honey," she said.

"I have something to tell you." Taking a deep breath, he sat down. "You know about those times I went to the casino. Well, I ended up losing thousands of dollars. I thought I could win it back, so I kept going. I used my credit cards to borrow the money. What I'm trying to say is, I owe so much money I have to claim bankruptcy."

There was a moment of silence. She just stared at him with a blank expression and closed the book she was reading.

"I'm going to claim individual bankruptcy, so it won't affect you or your savings," he said.

"It won't affect my credit," she said.

"No, just mine. I'll lose my credit cards, but I won't owe any more money."

"How could you do this, Jack?"

"I just got hooked, like an alcoholic. I thought I could win it back," he said. "We won't lose the house or anything. If you want, you can talk with my lawyer."

"So, how much did you lose?"

"You don't want to know."

"How much, Jack?"

"About forty thousand."

"Oh Jack…" She shook her head in disbelief.

"Don't worry, I still have my pension and some cash put away," he said, trying to calm her. "We'll be all right."

40
Christmas

The transit train to New York was making its morning run, passing by the bus yard.

Rossi was doing pushups between the seats. Rhythm and blues music came from the radio. The broken windows in the bus that were shot out by Dwayne were replaced by the company, and everything was clean and back to normal. He completed his exercise, then strapped himself into the driver's seat.

He drove slowly around to the monitor's lounge and met Alicia.

"Last day, then it's Christmas vacation time," she said, coming on the bus.

"Thank goodness. Are you having Christmas at home?" Rossi asked her.

"No, I'm eating at my parents' house."

"That's nice." He went a few blocks to his first stop. Several kids got on the bus and took seats.

"It feels like snow today," Alicia said.

"I hope not." Rossi hated the cold weather. When he retired, he wanted to move someplace warm. After a few more stops, they picked up one of the twins, Malcolm Thomas.

"How's your brother doing?" Rossi asked him.

"He's home from the hospital," Malcolm said. "He was in serious condition for awhile. Right now he has a big cast on his leg. My grandfather got your company to drop the charges, so he won't have to go to training school."

"Well, I hope he learned a lesson," Rossi said.

"He's sorry about trashing your bus," Malcolm said.

"I'm just the driver, it's not my bus," Rossi said as he drove along. A few snowflakes came down, hitting the ground and melting. Over the two-way, someone called the dispatcher for help.

"What's wrong?" Kenny asked the driver.

"I have a little girl just threw up her breakfast. Should I take her home or to school?"

"Take her home," Kenny answered.

"That's what I thought," the driver said.

Rossi let everyone off at school, then he did his elementary run.

While driving his Escort home that morning, he was wondering what to get Laurie for Christmas. She was still having some morning sickness and wasn't doing well with her legs. He stopped at a super drugstore and walked inside to the cosmetic section. He saw sets of cologne and thought they were nice. One had a hairbrush and comb with dusting power. He picked it up and had it gift wrapped.

Sadie met him at the door when he came home.

"Ross, come here a minute. I want you to meet someone."

He followed her into the kitchen.

"My son Rudy is here. I know you two have already met. I just want to thank you from the bottom of my heart," she said, smiling.

Her son was eating breakfast. He stood up, shaking Rossi's

hand. "Thanks, man," he said.

"Well, I'm glad you made it," Rossi said.

"Thank you," Sadie said, grinning from ear to ear. "How'd you find him?"

"I just got lucky," Rossi said.

"Would you like some breakfast?" Sadie asked him.

"No thanks, my girlfriend is waiting for me."

"This is going to be the best Christmas ever," Sadie said.

Rossi went upstairs and found her lying on the couch with her feet up on pillows.

"How are you feeling?" he said.

"Not so good," she said. "I threw up this morning."

"Do you need to see the doctor?"

"As long as I lay here, I'm all right," she said. "You could give me a glass of water and some Alka-seltzer."

After helping her, he made breakfast for himself and fed the cat. From the kitchen window, he could see snowflakes falling again. He turned on the television to get the weather report. They were forecasting light snow, maybe one or two inches.

"Do you want any coffee?" he asked her as he came into the room.

"Not right now," she said. "Maybe later."

"It's trying to snow," he said.

"Are we going to get much?"

"No, just enough to make it slippery outside."

On Saturday Laurie still wasn't feeling well, but on Christmas morning she was doing much better and the swelling around her ankles had gone down.

They had a small table tree with a star on top. Under the tree she found the gift from Rossi and carefully unwrapped it. When she saw the bath set, she was thrilled. She crept into the bedroom where he was sleeping and gave him an arousing kiss.

"Are you awake?" she asked.

"I am now," he said.

"Thank you for the gift," she said, kissing him again. "Now what would you like for Christmas?"

"Can I have a cup of coffee?" he said

"You can have anything you want," she said, smiling.

41
Going to Confession

Eva Gomez was doing her morning run. It was January, a new year and colder than ever. She wished she was lying on a warm beach in Puerto Rico. She stopped her bus, letting the monitor off to cross some kids. Suddenly, a speeding car approached them, slamming on its brakes. It skidded to a halt, just missing everyone.

The woman driving the car opened her window. "Sorry, I wasn't looking," she said. She was talking on her cell phone, then she blessed herself, making the sign of the cross.

When Eva returned home later, she found her son without any shoes on his feet. He was just wearing socks.

"How come you're not in school?" she said.

"I was robbed," he said. "I was waiting for the bus, when some big boys asked me for money. I told them I had none, so they took my shoes."

"Do you know these boys?" she asked.

"No, I never saw them before."

"I'm calling the police, but you still have to go to school. Go find your old shoes to wear."

"I don't know where they are," the boy said.

"Go find them and tonight I will buy you some new ones."

Miguel went into his room, looking through the closet, and

found a pair.

The police never showed up. Eva waited, but they never came, so she took her boy to school.

On the first Sunday of the month, a layer of snow covered the ground. Eva was getting ready for church. Her husband Luis dressed up and was going with them. He was still sleeping on the couch and wasn't too happy.

"I'm going to confession," he told her.

"You should go," she said, but she didn't believe him.

He went to start the car, brushing the snow from the windshield. When Eva came from the house with the children, Luis had the car ready and warm. Together, they rode to church.

They were early, taking seats near the front. Luis went into the confessional booth. Later, he sat with his family, holding his head down in prayer. He was trying to please his wife and gain her forgiveness. During the mass, he put five dollars in the collection basket, trying to make a good impression.

After it was over, he went with his family for breakfast. They entered the diner and took a table. Luis played a word game with the kids while they waited for the food. Eva just sat and drank her coffee.

"Do you want to play, Mommy?" Miguel tried to get her to play the game too.

"I don't feel like it," Eva said.

Their breakfast came and after they ate Luis paid the bill, making sure the waitress received a tip. On the way home, he promised to take the kids to see a movie later. For days he tried doing everything around the house to make Eva happy. He vacuumed the floors, washed the dishes, and even cleaned the toilet. One afternoon he surprised her by bringing home yellow roses.

"The flowers are nice," she said. She still had warm feelings for him, and he was the father of their three children.

"My back is killing me from sleeping on the couch," he told her.

"Well, what are you sleeping there for…?" she said, smiling with her eyes.

42
Snow Busing

The forecast was for three inches of snow. Rossi put on his baseball cap, then his coat and gloves. He glanced out the window from his house.

"It's snowing pretty good," he said. "I think you better stay home this afternoon."

"I am, my legs are bothering me," Laurie said.

"Well, I'm going."

"Be careful," she said.

The wind was blowing hard. He started his Escort and cleared the windows. He had front-wheel drive and getting to work was no problem.

When he came to Turner Yard, the buses were running with clouds of gray fumes filling the air. He found his and started it, turning on the heat. Using a broom, he went outside and brushed away the snow from around the mirrors and front hood. His face was frozen by the time he finished.

He drove around the building to get Alicia, but she wasn't there. Most of the monitors stayed home because of the snow. The traffic was slow and cars were stuck by the side of the road.

He arrived at the school late and noticed the sidewalks around the grounds were never shoveled. The students made their way through the snow. Two of the boys started a snowball fight. The principal had to come over and ordered them on the bus.

When Rossi left the school with the bus, it was like a blizzard. The wind was blowing the snow into the windshield, and he had trouble driving from one street to another. The kids riding the bus weren't concerned; they just wanted to hear loud music from the radio.

It took him longer, but somehow he managed to finish the first run and get to the second school. A few of the parents were waiting in cars to take their kids home. A teacher led the elementary kids from the building.

"How are the roads?" she asked him.

"It's bad," Rossi said.

"Where are the other buses?"

"They should be coming."

Some of the little kids were excited with all the snow. They were sliding their feet in it and falling on their backs.

"C'mon, get on the bus," the teacher said.

After the children were seated, Rossi stood and talked to them. "Listen up. This is a bad storm, so I don't want any fooling around. Okay? Everyone hear me?"

"Okay Ross, we'll be good," someone said. The other children nodded their heads in response.

Probably fifty percent of the drivers on the road had never seen snow. They came from other countries like Mexico and had no experience with driving in winter weather. People with bald tires were having trouble and getting stuck.

Rossi tried his best to get the kids home. Driving a big bus through the snow was like threading a needle with a marshmallow. When he opened the door, the wind was so bad, it blew the snow right up the stairs. Cars were crawling along no faster than snails.

It took him forever to go a couple of blocks, where he let two more kids out.

"You go right home," he told them.

Ahead of them, a car was stranded in the middle of the street with no driver. He managed to steer around it. He couldn't believe how fast it was coming down. Several inches were already on the ground. Suddenly there was a large rumble of thunder that frightened some of the kids on the bus. They covered their ears with their hands and closed their eyes.

"Dispatcher, this is sixty-two."

"What's the problem?" Kenny asked.

"We're stuck on Congress Street," the driver said. "There's too much snow and we can't move."

"Stand by, I'll see if I can get a city plow over there," Kenny said.

"Well, we're not going anywhere," the driver said.

Everyone was having problems. Rossi was trying to get to his next stop. The streets were so bad, it was impossible for some cars to move. He kept driving through the snow and it was getting late. He counted fourteen kids left on the bus.

Little Joanna began to cry. "I want to go home," she said. A bigger girl tried to calm her.

"I'm gonna miss my supper," Big Ben moaned.

The side mirrors on the bus were icing up. He pulled over and went outside with an ice scraper. The snow was blinding, stinging his eyes and cheeks as he cleaned the mirrors.

"Are we stuck?" Big Ben asked him when he came back inside the bus.

"Not yet," Rossi said

A line of cars were blocking the road ahead, so he turned into a side street, going up a hill. Before getting to the top, the bus wheels started slipping. He had to back down slowly to the bottom. Shifting the gears from third to second, he headed up the hill again. This time the bus made it.

He went a block and turned up another road. He was trying to get back on his route, but the snow was too deep for the wheels and the bus wouldn't move anymore.

"Are we stuck?" Big Ben asked again.

"Looks that way," Rossi said.

"Then let me go. I'll walk home." Ben stood up.

"I can't let you go. It's bad out there, so sit down," Rossi ordered him.

"I wanna go home and eat my supper," Ben said.

"If anything happens to you, I'd lose my job," Rossi said. "Now listen to me, we have to stick together and wait here until we get help. You understand?" The children looked at him with hopeless faces.

He called the dispatcher and reported his position.

"How long are we gonna be here?" Charlie Simpson asked. His good eye had a nervous twitch.

"I don't know," Rossi said, turning the radio dial to hear the news. The weatherman said the storm was stalled over the city, dropping record amounts of snow, and the wind chill was in the teens.

It was getting dark outside. Rossi had to keep the bus running with the heat on to keep everyone warm. He focused his eyes on the fuel gauge. There was less than a quarter of a tank. If they didn't get help soon, they could freeze to death. He walked through the bus, wondering what to do. He peeked through the back window, seeing two cars already stuck behind them. There was no place to go. He went to his seat and waited.

"I'm hungry," Big Ben said.

"I am too," Rossi said.

"Attention, Providence buses," Kenny announced over the two-way. "I want all buses to return to the yard. Do not attempt to bring anyone else home. The roads are too bad, so bring the kids back here. If you're stuck in the snow, you have to wait for help."

"Rossi, we're never gonna get home," Big Ben complained again.

"We have to wait here. Just close your eyes and rest. Pretend you're on a warm tropical island," Rossi said.

"Yeah, right," Ben said. "An island with lots of coconuts and bananas to eat." He licked his lips. He was being funny and the kids laughed at him.

It was completely dark now and some of the children fell asleep. Rossi left the bus running to keep the heat going. The fuel was getting lower. Maybe they forgot where the bus was, Rossi thought. He called the yard again.

"This is nineteen. We're running out of fuel. Is the plow coming soon?" he said.

"The plows are working as fast as they can. We can't do anything else. You'll just have to wait," Kenny said.

"Ten-four," Rossi said.

"Ross, this is Jack. I'm stuck about four blocks from you on Lowell Avenue with plenty of fuel and a heated bus, if you can walk this way."

"Thanks for the invitation, Jack. I'll be getting back to you soon. Keep your ears open," Rossi said.

The news on the radio wasn't good. It was a freak storm. Cars were being abandoned by the hundreds and people were walking home, even the snow plows were having trouble. Rossi went around inside the bus, checking on the sleeping kids, making sure their jackets were zipped up. Charlie Simpson was still awake.

"Are we gonna be here all night?" he asked.

"Help should be coming pretty soon," he said, going back to his seat to think. The engine was still running even though the fuel gauge was on empty.

He tried shutting the bus off for awhile. When it started to get cold inside again, he turned it on, letting it warm up. He kept gazing through the window for a plow to come, but didn't see anything. Before long the engine sputtered and stalled.

They just couldn't sit there any longer and freeze to death. He knew he had to do something.

"Kenny, do you copy?" Rossi asked.

"I copy," Kenny answered.

"I ran out of fuel and we can't wait here. It's too cold, so I'm taking the kids to meet bus fifty-eight if he's still there."

"Fifty-eight, are you there?" Kenny asked.

"I'm still here," Jack said.

"Nineteen is walking his kids your way," Kenny said.

Rossi had to get the kids ready.

"Wake up! Everyone wake up. It's time to go," he told them. "We can't stay here because it's too cold. We have to walk to another bus."

"How far is it?" Ben asked.

"It's not far. Make sure you wear your mittens and hats. You bigger kids, take the little ones by the hand and don't let go. Ben, I want you to be last in line. You have to make sure that no one is left behind." Rossi picked up Joanna and carried her in his arms. She was small and didn't weigh much. "Let's go. Follow me," he said. "Everyone hold hands so you don't get lost."

There was a lull in the storm and the wind died down; Rossi knew it was time to go. He padded the snow down with his shoes, making a path for them to follow. He kept checking around him, making sure everyone was following in line. Ben, who was carrying a little boy, brought up the rear.

"I'm freezing," Charlie Simpson said.

"Keep going!" Rossi barked like a drill sergeant. "Keep going. Don't stop!"

They stepped through the snow. The few blocks seemed like miles. Finally, Rossi could see dim lights ahead of them. "There's the bus!" he shouted. "We're almost there."

Jack appeared at the door as they came closer. "Welcome to School Bus Hilton," he said, brushing the snow off them as they came up the steps. The children stumbled inside and found a seat; they were happy to be on a warm bus.

"Am I glad to see you," Rossi said, catching his breath.

"Glad to be of service." Jack had three small kids with him and no monitor.

"This storm is bad," Rossi said.

"Looks like ten inches of snow," Jack said.

"I can't believe it," Rossi said, rubbing his cold hands together.

"It's never gonna stop," Ben said, sitting a few rows back. He could see a lighted building in the distance. "Is that a store up the road?"

"It looks like one," Jack said.

"Man, am I hungry," Ben said.

"Me too," Charlie Simpson said.

"As soon as I get warm, I'll go check it out," Rossi said. "Maybe we can get something to eat."

PASSING THROUGH PROVIDENCE

"All right!" Ben said, his eyes growing brighter.

"You did good, Ben, carrying that kid," Rossi said.

"I did?" Ben smiled.

"Yes, you did," Rossi acknowledged.

"Then can I go with you to the store? I have my own money," Ben said.

"Of course you can, but we have to get warm first," Rossi said.

"You think we're going to be here all night?" Jack said.

"Who knows, maybe," Rossi said.

After awhile, Ben was getting impatient. "Are you ready to go now?" he said.

"Hold down the fort, Jack, we're going." Rossi went outside up to his knees in snow and Ben followed him.

They trudged along and the wind started to blow hard again.

"Boy, this stuff is deep," Ben said.

"I hope this place is open," Rossi said, approaching the store.

Ben could see someone through the window. "There's a man inside." He tried the door and it wouldn't move. "Oh no," the boy moaned. He pushed it harder until it opened.

"I was getting ready to close," the man said. "I ran out of milk and I'm almost out of bread."

"Well, I'm glad you didn't," Rossi said, looking around. "We're stuck in a school bus and the kids are hungry."

He took the last three loaves of bread, some peanut butter and jelly, bags of chips, and candy. He put everything on the counter. "Okay, this should do it."

"We need a knife to make sandwiches," Ben said.

"I have no knives, only this," the man held up a plastic spoon.

"We can scoop it on the bread," Rossi said.

"I'll buy this," Ben said, holding a big bag of popcorn and a chocolate bar.

"Here you go," Rossi said, pulling a twenty dollar bill from his wallet.

The man put everything into a paper bag, plus an extra bag of chips. "That's on me," he said.

"Thank you very much," Rossi said, getting his change.

They went outside into the wind and snow and followed their tracks back. Coming inside the bus, Jack turned on the dome lights so they could see. Rossi sat down, opening the jars of peanut butter and jelly, making sandwiches for everyone. The kids ate as if they were starving. Nothing was wasted; even the chip bags were quickly emptied.

Rossi opened the bag of candy. "Two pieces each," he said.

Anything to drink," someone said.

"This isn't a restaurant," Jack said. "If you're thirsty, get a handful of snow and lick it."

Some of the kids liked the idea. They went outside for minute and picked up a handful of snow to eat. Giggling and licking the snow, they hurried back on the bus.

It was getting late and everyone was tired. Jack turned off the lights, but kept the engine running to keep it warm inside.

Rossi played his harmonica and most of the kids fell asleep.

A few hours passed before a plow came down the street. Its lights were shining like a battleship as it came to their rescue, clearing the way so they could move.

"We came to get you out," the plow guy said.

"You're my hero," Jack said as he drove away.

It was almost midnight when they arrived at Turner Yard.

Everyone was glad to leave the bus and go inside the building. Hundreds of children were sitting on the floor and some were sleeping on blankets. There was lots of hot chocolate to drink and plenty of donuts to eat, putting smiles on all the kids' faces.

Rossi called Laurie on the phone, hoping she was still awake. "Were you asleep?" he asked.

"No, I was watching television. Where are you?"

"Our bus was stuck in the snow for hours. We just made it back to the yard. The snow is too deep, so I'll be staying here with the kids until morning."

"Well, I'm glad you're safe. I called the dispatcher and he told me you were stuck and couldn't get out," she said.

"Well, don't worry. Get some sleep," he said. "I have to go now, someone else wants to use the phone."

"Bye, sweetie," she said.

The next day the weather was better with only a few light flurries. The ground was covered with over a foot of snow and the drifts were up to six feet high. The National Guard was called to help plow the roads. School was closed and the children were happy to be going home.

43
The American Way

Jack attended a few meetings for Gamblers Anonymous the past month. He took his wife to dinner a few times and even went bowling once.

His court day came in February. He dressed in a gray suit and tie and drove to Providence. He hated going downtown, because finding a parking space was like finding a box of fifty dollar bills. He drove through the city for twenty minutes before he found a place.

The bankruptcy court was located on the eighth floor of a bank building. He was right on time and met his young lawyer in the hallway. She gave him some instructions.

"I want you to remain calm and answer any questions the judge might have for you," she said.

"How long does this take?" Jack asked her.

"About an hour. Don't worry, everything will be all right," she said.

He followed her into a large room filled with chairs. There were about twenty people waiting. The judge was sitting at a long desk facing everyone. He was wearing a plain suit and looked like a businessman. He was doing paperwork, checking some documents. Jack took a seat with his lawyer.

Before long, the judge was ready. He told everyone to stand

and hold up their right hand, pledging an oath to tell the truth. The judge waited until everyone was seated again, then he called someone's name. A man stood up and the judge asked him several questions about his bills and other things. When the judge was through, he signed some papers and stamped them.

Jack's name was called next. He stood and answered a few questions. The proceedings didn't take long. Everyone went through the same process, until the last person was done, followed by a long period of silence in the room as the judge did his paperwork.

When they were dismissed, everyone was glad to go. Jack strolled down the hallway feeling relieved, like he'd gone to church and confessed his sins. When the door opened for the elevator, everyone from the courtroom crowded inside. On the way down, one guy was smiling. "Eighty thousand in bills gone, just like that!" he said, snapping his fingers.

"It's the American way," another man said.

Jack left the building and walked along the street. He saw a picture of a large cruise ship in the window. It was a travel agency. His wife always wanted to go on a Caribbean cruise, so he stopped to inquire.

Inside the office, a nice woman told him more about the ship. He reached into his pocket, pulling out a big roll of hundreds, and paid for the cruise in cash.

He was going home to surprise his wife. Everything in his life was better now, except for one thing…he was still dreaming about the damn mail.

44
Lucky Ticket

It was Drivers Appreciation Day. Management was serving breakfast in the lounge. The smell of bacon and sausage made everyone hungry. Several large tins filled with food were trucked in by a local caterer. Extra fold-up tables were set in place with chairs, so everyone had a place to eat.

Kenny was pouring coffee into cups and Linda Stevens was serving scrambled eggs. "Here you go, eat up and don't forget the biscuits," she was saying. Most of the drivers went back for seconds, then later they sat around and talked about their daily lives. One of them was all excited about getting married in Jamaica and everyone was listening to her. She was going to spend several days there with her new husband. It was her third marriage in five years.

February vacation came the following week. Eva and Luis packed their bags and took their children to the Cape in Massachusetts. Luis was sleeping with his wife again and wanted his family to have a nice time.

It wasn't a long drive. They went over the Sagamore Bridge and down the road to Hyannis. Motels and fast-food restaurants lined the streets of the town. Late in the afternoon, Luis pulled the car into a motel. He had reservations and went into the office for the room key.

It was a large place with a nice indoor swimming pool. They could see some kids playing in the water.

"Is this where we are staying?" Miguel asked.

"This is it," Eva said.

"Mommy, I want to go swimming," her oldest daughter said.

"You have to wait," Eva said.

Luis came back and drove the car around the side of the building where they unloaded their bags. The room where they were staying had two large queen-size beds and a colored television with a nice large bathroom.

The children had their swimsuits on in minutes. They were ready for the pool. Eva unpacked, hanging the clothes in the closet. She opened the dresser drawers and put some things in there too.

Luis brought a cooler packed with soda and beer. He turned on the television and opened a brew for himself.

"Are you going swimming, Mom?" Miguel was tired of waiting.

When Eva was ready, she marched the kids down the hallway. The water was heated and the kids couldn't wait to jump into the pool.

Eva found the hot tub in the corner and sank into the steamy water up to her chest. She felt relaxed sitting there. It was nice of Luis to take them to the Cape. It was their first time there and the kids were enjoying it.

After awhile, she joined the kids in the pool. They played swimming games until they were tired, then they went back to the room and watched television.

Luis was the first one up first in the morning. He dressed and went down the hallway to the lobby for some coffee, juice, and donuts. He carried everything back to the room on a tray and placed it on a table. The kids were hungry and helped themselves.

When Miguel was dressed, he asked, "What are we doing today, Mommy?"

"We're going to the mall," she said.

"To the mall, oh boy!" Miguel said.

As soon as the kids finished all the donuts, they were ready. They went outside in the cold morning air, getting into the car.

"Wait a minute," Eva said. She forgot her coat and went back to get it. It was still winter and she didn't need to catch a cold

Riding in the car, Eva spotted a Christmas shop. "Let's stop there," she said.

They walked inside and found a thousand different items. Patio furniture, books, toys, and packaged food were only a few of them. After spending some time there, she purchased some cooking utensils and potholders. Her kids wanted something, but they couldn't make up their minds, so she told them to wait until later.

They went to the mall next, a mile down the road. It was school vacation and most of the shoppers had their children with them. They had a variety of stores there, even a food court with pizza, hamburgers, and ice cream. At the candy store, Luis purchased a box of chocolates for his wife and some gumdrops for the kids.

Eva saw a ladies outlet and went inside to check the undergarments on sale. Instead of waiting for her, Luis took the kids to a toy store. They wanted him to buy everything on the shelves. Hoping to make them happy, he bought each of them a toy of their choice.

"Can we go back to the motel and go swimming now?" Miguel asked.

"It's too early," Luis told them.

When Eva found them, she was carrying a bag of new clothes.

PASSING THROUGH PROVIDENCE

"I want to see the monkeys," one of the girls said.

"Okay, let's go see the monkeys at the pet store," Eva said, putting her hand in her coat pocket. "What's this?" She felt something and pulled out two scratch tickets she forgot she had. "Where did these come from?"

She thought back for a minute, remembering the day she saw the beautiful rainbow. It was a few months ago and she was talking with Rossi. She rubbed the spots off the tickets. "Look at this, I won a hundred dollars," she said.

"You did," Luis said. "Let me see the ticket."

"I had it in my pocket all this time."

"Is it still good?" Luis asked her.

"Yes, they're good for a year," she said. She was surprised she'd won the money. "When I bought the tickets, I saw this beautiful rainbow and it was my lucky day, but I didn't know it until now." She checked the other ticket.

"Oh my God!" she gasped, turning white. She felt like she was going to faint.

"Now what?" Luis said.

"Oh my God!" she said again, showing him the ticket.

"How much is it?"

"Do you see?" she cried.

His eyes grew bigger. "I can't believe it, five thousand dollars!"

45
Hijacked Bus

Laurie examined her stomach. She was in her seventh month and was beginning to show. Her belly was shaped like a half moon and her doctor gave her a clean bill of health. Her morning sickness had gone away and she was able to continue her job as a monitor. She needed to save some money for the baby.

One day in March, she stepped from the school bus and led the children across the street. While getting back on the bus, someone grabbed her from behind and shoved her up the stairs.

He was a tall man with a black beard. He pulled a knife and held it to her throat. "Get off the bus!" he shouted at the driver.

When Laurie heard his voice, she knew it was her former husband. "Alex, what are you doing?" she said.

"I said get off the bus or I'll cut her open!" He pressed the knife harder against her skin. The driver didn't know what to do, so he left the bus.

"Let the kids go too," Laurie begged him. There were four youngsters and one of them started to cry.

"Okay, get the hell away from here," he yelled at them. The children stood up and ran outside to freedom.

"What are you doing, Alex?" He had dark circles around his bloodshot eyes and had grown a beard.

"Sit down, sweetheart," he said, pushing her. He slid the knife in his belt, sitting himself behind the driver's wheel.

"You must be on drugs!" Laurie shouted.

"I was released early." He looked like he was high on something. He put the bus in gear.

"You can't drive this bus," she said.

"I drove a truck before. Nothing to it," he said.

"Yeah, right."

"For the last couple of days, I've been watching you."

"We're no longer married and you know it."

"That divorce you got was a big mistake." He went faster, driving through a red light, almost hitting a car.

"Slow down," she said.

"You married me for better or worse, remember?" He was driving all over the road.

"Will you slow down!" She couldn't believe how fast he was going. Good thing there was a seatbelt. She put the straps together and buckled it over her lap, holding onto the seat.

After a few breathless minutes, she heard Kenny on the two-way radio. "Be on the lookout for bus eight. It was hijacked with the monitor. Do not pursue, just let me know if you see it."

"Bus eight is going down Elmwood Avenue away from the city," someone responded.

"Alex, you better slow down," Laurie warned him again.

Rossi was driving his empty bus when he heard Kenny. He knew Laurie was on that bus the last couple of days. He stepped on the accelerator, taking a shortcut. He was just minutes from Elmwood Avenue and had to get there fast.

Suddenly a police car with lights flashing came up from behind, speeding around him. He slowed down for a moment, then watched as the patrol car disappeared down the road. When he came to Elmwood Avenue, another police car passed him. He followed them down the road, driving the bus as fast as possible. Some cars were in the way and he blew the horn going by them. He could see the police ahead catching up to the hijacked bus.

Then it happened: the bus crashed into a tractor trailer.

The collision was so loud, Rossi could hear it. The truck went through an intersection and slammed into the front of the bus where the driver sat. Parts of metal scattered over the ground. Rossi stopped his bus on the side of the road and jumped out, running as fast as he could. Red flames were shooting up from the truck and someone was tugging at the bus door. Fuel was leaking everywhere and the fire was beginning to spread.

"Where are you going?" a police officer asked him.

"My girlfriend's in there!" Rossi shouted, rushing to the back of the bus. He opened the emergency door and climbed inside, moving through the smoke to the front. The driver wasn't moving and looked dead. He was bleeding badly and his head was smashed through the windshield.

Laurie lay unconscious, slumped in her seat. A huge bump was on her forehead and blood was coming from her nose. He unhooked her seatbelt, carrying her to the back of the bus, then the police officer helped him get her to safety.

Minutes later, a fire truck pulled up, but it was too late for the bearded guy. Flames were shooting up everywhere. A rescue truck came and the crew carried Laurie on a stretcher.

At St. Joseph's Hospital the following day, Rossi and Laurie's brother Danny stood next to her bed. She was resting in a coma. A doctor came in the room and examined her.

"Is she going to be all right?" Rossi asked him.

PASSING THROUGH PROVIDENCE

"I don't know. She really banged her head," the doctor said. "She's breathing okay. We just have to watch her for now."

Her brother was holding her hand. "Wake up, Laurie," he said.

"She's seven months pregnant," Rossi told the doctor.

"Really." The doctor seemed surprised. "She doesn't show it."

"Can she hear me?" her brother asked the doctor.

"I'm not sure, maybe. I'll be back later to check on her." He left the room.

"Wake up, Laurie," her brother kept repeating, but she didn't move.

The two of them waited hopelessly by her bedside for a couple of hours. Rossi blamed himself; he knew he should have stopped her from working. Later, he went to get some coffee. He searched the hallways for a snack bar and became lost.

By accident, he found the chapel. He thought it was faith that led him there, and he couldn't believe his eyes at what he saw. It was small, but in some way, magnificent. On the altar was a cross of Jesus. There were several rows of pews, so he knelt down on his knees, blessing himself. He whispered his prayers, hoping Laurie would get better. He promised to be more religious and help those in need. Standing up again, he forgot about the coffee and returned to her room. Her brother was gone and she was alone.

"Laurie, I love you," he said, then noticed the silver cross. It was on a fine chain around her neck. He thought it was odd that he didn't see it earlier. He rubbed the cross with his forefinger and tears filled his eyes. After awhile, he grew tired and sat in a chair nearby. His head drooped toward the floor and he closed his eyes.

Sometime later, a sudden brightness came into the room. The cross she was wearing glittered from the sunlight through the window. Her face moved and her eyes slowly opened. "Ross," she said, confused.

He lifted his head in disbelief. "Laurie, you're awake."

"Where am I?"

"You're in the hospital," he said, hugging her.

"I'm so thirsty," she managed to say.

He was glad to hear her voice again. He pushed the buttons, one for the nurse and one to raise her headboard. He gave her some water with a straw to drink. The nurse came and was surprised to see her sitting up.

After talking with her, Rossi went to call her brother, giving him the good news.

The following morning, he came back to see her. She looked fine and was drinking orange juice.

"Hi, Ross," she said as he came in the room.

"I'm glad you're doing better."

"The doctor wants to keep me here a little longer. My head is sore, but I feel okay."

"Did you have any breakfast?"

"Some eggs," she said.

Putting her hand over her stomach, she said, "Oh my."

"What's the matter?" he asked.

"The baby's kicking," she said. "Put your hand here." He laid his hand on her stomach.

"Wow," he said.

"Oh no," she said.

"Now what's the matter?"

"My water just broke. The baby's coming!"

Rossi ran to get a nurse.

PART II

46
Spring Again

In the spring, the squirrels were playing again and the birds were singing, while the street cats were hiding in the bushes, eying their prey.

Rossi did his school bus runs each day and came home to Laurie and her baby. She gave birth prematurely to a tiny baby girl and they named her Anna.

"How's she doing?" Rossi asked.

"She's kicking her little legs and drawling all over herself," Laurie said. "And I'm gonna need some more diapers and formula from the store."

"I'll go later," he said. He went to the bedroom, changing his clothes and putting on his sweats. He did some exercises on the floor.

Tommy Boy came from under the bed and stretched his body. "Meoww."

"You hungry, boy?" He went to the kitchen and the cat followed him. He opened a can of tuna, putting it into a dish on the floor for him. The cat pounced on it like it was his last meal.

Rossi went outside where his front lawn was turning greener by the day, then he jogged down the street. With the warmer weather, some of his neighbors were painting and fixing up their houses. It was good to see people taking an interest in their property.

When he came to Mt. Pleasant High School, he was tired and started to walk. He was finding it harder with age to keep up a good pace.

Returning home, Sadie Smith was taking a bag of garbage to the trash can.

"How's Laurie and the baby doing?" she asked him.

"Oh, they're fine. I'm going to the store this morning. Do you need anything?"

"Let's see, I need some eggs. I'll give you a list."

"I'll be going soon," he told her, then went into the house.

Laurie was feeding the baby with a bottle.

"After I shower, I'm going to the store," he said.

"Don't forget the diapers and formula," she said.

Just having her and the baby in the house made him happy. He liked being a family man and doing things for her.

After bringing home the groceries and things for Laurie and Sadie, Rossi went back to work. He had to do his afternoon run. He entered his bus and found no key. He checked everywhere for it, across the dashboard and over the radio. He knew someone used the bus, but why take the key? He went to the dispatcher's office and told Kenny.

"Did you look over the radio?" Kenny asked him.

"I checked everywhere," Rossi said.

"I'll have to give you the spare key." Kenny looked into a box for a couple of minutes and found one. "Here you go."

Rossi was on his way to the door when he noticed the coffeepot half full. There were plenty of extra paper cups, powered milk, and sugar, so he poured himself a cup.

The TV was on and no one was watching it. He heard a group

of drivers who were sitting around a table talking about their friend who was fired.

"He worked here for twenty years."

"What happened to him?"

"He hit a car in the rear with the bus."

"Was anyone hurt?"

"No one was hurt, little damage."

"Then he should have been suspended, not fired."

Rossi couldn't believe it either. He walked back to his bus carrying his coffee. Someone must have taken his broom, because it was gone, but it didn't matter; he had another one in the back. He sat in the driver's seat and tried the key. It wouldn't turn. He kept pushing it with his fingers. Finally, it clicked over and started the engine. The fuel gauge was on empty. Somebody really went for a long drive, he thought.

He pulled the bus up to the pump and no one was there.

"Kenny, this is Ross, I need fuel," he called over the two-way.

"You don't have enough to do a run?" Kenny sounded irritated.

"No, someone used my bus and left it empty," Rossi answered.

"Just a minute, I'll get somebody."

Finally, he picked up Alicia with the bus.

"I thought you were never coming," she said.

"I had to get fuel."

They went up to Union Avenue, where the traffic was bad for some reason.

"So how's things at home?" she asked him.

"Just fine."

When they came to the middle school, the kids were waiting

on the sidewalk. Rossi opened the door and everyone pushed their way onto the bus.

"You're late," Easy Lucy said, chewing her gum. She found a seat next to some boys.

The Thomas twins were there too, still bickering, but not fighting. JoVon was gone; he'd moved away.

"Can you put the music on?" Easy Lucy said.

"Can you say 'please'?" Rossi responded.

"Please, please," Lucy said twice.

He turned on the radio, hoping the kids would be good, and drove down the road, letting a few of them off. A new boy on the bus was being loud. Alicia had to tell him to be quiet. Rossi always felt better after the twins left, because they were the most trouble. When the bus was empty, they went to the elementary school.

A teacher brought the kids from the building in a single line. One by one, they hopped up the stairs.

"You're the last bus here," the teacher said.

"I know, I had some problems," Rossi told her.

On the way home, some of the kids were tired and fell asleep. Big Ben was awake, eating a bag of chips and humming to himself. Crazy Eyes was showing Carlos his video game. A few of the girls were reading their books.

Rossi was thinking, I hope these kids get good jobs when they grow up and pay into Social Security, so I can get a check when I retire.

47
A Good Wife

Boris Tolchek parked his bus in front of his house. He made thousands of dollars from the stock market and owned two buses now. He bought the empty lot across the street to park his buses and had a wire fence put around it with a wide gate.

For some reason, he was feeling horny when he entered his house. He found his wife still in her bathrobe and washing dishes in the kitchen.

Mary heard him coming. "Oh, it's you, I thought it was the milkman," she giggled.

He gave her a hug. "How about some sugar?" he said, kissing her on the neck, then he picked her up in his strong arms, all hundred and fifty pounds, and carried her into the bedroom.

In the afternoon, he took her on the small bus for a ride.
"I want you to learn how to drive a bus," he said
"Drive the bus!" she said, surprised.
"Yeah, you can do it."
"You think so?"
"Sure, I'll teach you. You have a driver's license, right?"
"For a car," she said.
"No problem."
He drove the bus from the city to a deserted street where there

was a large dirt field, then let her take the wheel.

It wasn't long before she and Boris were both doing charters. She was gaining more confidence with the smaller bus every day. She was glad she had something to do besides sitting around the house. She started doing the checking account and was good with figures. She was amazed to see how much they were making. Before she met her husband, she'd gone out with a few guys; however, none of them wanted to settle down. Boris was willing to get married, but he didn't want any kids until later, so she had to take birth control pills.

Boris kept his prices low because he was competing with the Turner Bus Company. Between the schools and the churches, they were getting enough work to keep the two of them busy.

The new bus was bigger. On a weekday, he took it with a load of kids from a private school to downtown Providence. They had several adults with them and they were going to see a play at Trinity Theater. He dropped them next to the theater and agreed to pick them up later.

They went to visit her parents one afternoon. Boris didn't like her father, but he went anyway. Her father was a retired railroad worker on disability and liked to talk; her mother never said much.

"How's the business doing?" her father asked her. He was a large man with gray hair.

"We're keeping busy. Boris likes to make money," she said.

"Well, that's good. When are you going to have kids? You know, little Ruskies?"

"Don't be funny, Dad. If I had any kids, they'd be Americans."

"Little Ruskies," he said again, being ridiculous.

Her mother served cookies and coffee, and after a few hours, Boris was glad to leave.

48
Cruising Time

Jack took a leave of absence from work and flew down to Tampa, Florida, with his wife and boarded the ship around lunchtime. Betty packed her luggage with her best clothes; she couldn't believe she was going on a cruise.

A photographer took their pictures when they arrived, and the photos would be available tomorrow. It was a huge majestic ship. They took the elevator and walked down elegant corridors with plush carpets to their cabin.

"I'm sorry, I couldn't get one with a balcony," Jack said.

"This is all right, honey. We have a TV, refrigerator, and a bathroom with a shower," she said.

"Good, I'm glad you like it. Now let's get something to eat." He was hungry because they didn't have any breakfast.

A room steward gave them directions to the buffet. They found it near the rear of the ship. The food looked fabulous. Everyone took a tray and helped themselves. There were several serving counters filled with meats and vegetables and a cheese table. Mary was delighted with the different kinds of salad.

"I finally get to go on a cruise," she said.

"Isn't this great," Jack said, cutting his meat.

"This cheese is so good," Betty said.

When they finished, she sipped her coffee and Jack drank

a beer.

An hour later, the ship pulled away from the dock. The whistle blew as everyone stood near the railing waving their good-byes. Jack and Betty were standing on the top deck watching as the ship moved into the harbor.

"We're on our way," Betty said.

Jack put his arm around his wife and gave her a kiss.

After they lost sight of land, they went back to their cabin. She unpacked their luggage and put the clothes into a set of drawers near the wall. She'd brought along some bottles of spring water to drink, putting them into the fridge.

Jack turned on the TV. One channel was giving information about the cruise, and there was something about an evacuation drill.

"We have to be ready," Jack said.

"For what?" Betty asked him.

"The safety drill."

"We have to do it?"

"Yes."

"Are you kidding me?"

"No, I'm not. Everyone has to do it." There were a couple of orange vests in the room. He pulled them out and read the directions.

"I'd like to take a shower first," Betty said.

"You don't have time." Jack glanced at his watch.

Within minutes, the alarm sounded and everyone hurried into the corridor wearing their orange life vests. They went outside on deck and waited before receiving instructions from a crew member. He told them how to wear their vests properly and how to abandon ship in a lifeboat.

"I hope we never have to do this," someone said.

"I hope we never have to do it either," the crew member said.

And everyone had a good laugh.

The next day, the photo shop had everyone's picture on the wall. Jack found theirs and showed it to Betty. She didn't like it.

"You look like a drunk, and I look like I gained a few pounds," she said.

He bought it anyway. The sales lady placed it into a souvenir folder for them, then they went to the gift shop where there was everything from expensive rum cakes to toys.

"Oh, I like these," Betty said. She found some T-shirts with the ship's name on them and bought them for the kids.

Jack noticed the high-priced bottles of liquor in one section. Too much money for me, he thought.

They went into several other shops before returning to their cabin. Jack was tired of standing, so he lay down to watch TV and fell asleep.

Betty sat in an easy chair and read her new novel for an hour. Close to dinnertime, she dressed and put some fresh makeup on her face. She had to wake Jack up and gave him a nudge with her hand.

"C'mon, we have to get ready," she said.

He slowly opened his eyes to make sure he wasn't dreaming. He sat up feeling better.

"What time is it?" he asked.

"Our seating time is six-thirty, so we have thirty minutes," she said.

"Okay, I just have to put on a tie and jacket." A minute later, he was ready.

They found their way there. The large dining room was filled with well-dressed people sitting at tables and being served by busy young waiters prancing among them.

There were six couples to a table and they were the last two seated.

Everyone had a choice of meals: first came the salad, then the main course, and later dessert. Betty ordered a class of wine and Jack a brew.

An older couple seated at their table was from Canada. "This is our fifth cruise," the man said. "We drive our RV down to Florida every year and leave it in a trailer park."

After eating, Betty wiped her mouth with her fancy napkin. She was quite satisfied with her dinner. Jack had a large steak and was full.

"That was good," she said, finishing with the lemon meringue pie.

"It was good," Jack said, "but I'd rather go to the buffet."

It wasn't long before everyone parted, saying their good-byes.

Jack took his wife's hand and headed for the theater, for it was almost show time. Because the ship was so big, they had to be careful of which way they were going. They took the gold-polished elevator up to a different level and stepped out, walking a short time. They followed signs that directed them, before they found the theater. Getting there was fun, like going on an adventure.

There were hundreds of people already sitting in rows. They took a seat and caught their breath. Minutes later, the lights turned down, the stage curtain opened, and young ladies appeared, dancing and singing with the music. There were several group songs performed with guys, and some of the girls sang solo.

PASSING THROUGH PROVIDENCE

Halfway through the show, there was a short intermission for everyone. Jack was glad, because he had to pee twenty minutes ago

The curtain came up again and the entertainment continued with the same performers for another half hour or so. Jack saw a musical in New York City once; this show had to be a close second.

"That was wonderful," Betty said when it was over.

"I'm glad you liked it," Jack said. "Let's go for a drink."

It wasn't long before they found themselves sitting at a cozy table in a darkened lounge. The bartender was putting on a show, flipping bottles through the air. Everyone there gave him a hand, then the lights started changing colors and a small band began playing music. Couples moved to the center of the floor, slow dancing.

Jack took his wife's hand, keeping with the rhythm of the music, and they stepped around with the crowd. As they moved, he noticed a lot of older couples dancing and having a good time. It's nice to retire and enjoy yourself, he thought. When the band stopped playing, everyone returned to their drinks.

After a late night, they headed back to their cabin. They went down the wrong corridor and were lost again.

"I think we had too much to drink," Betty said, laughing.

49
A New House

Eva Gomez loved her new house. She made the down payment with the money she won from the lucky ticket and bought a triple-decker in Cranston. She figured two of the rents would cover the mortgage and taxes and they could live for free. The first floor had three bedrooms, a nice kitchen, and a large living room and happened to be empty, so she moved in with her family. Her husband Luis was happy too, especially with the big yard for the kids to play in.

The second floor was smaller and occupied by a middle-aged man, and the third by a retired lady. Eva liked the new neighborhood; she thought the schools were better too.

One day she wanted to go shopping at a big grocery store on Elmwood Avenue. She went there with Luis and bought two carts full of everything she needed. She felt she could afford it now, since she was living for free.

"I have to get a bigger car," Luis said, packing the bags into the trunk and backseat.

In the morning she went back to work and found her bus missing. Kenny told her it was taken for state inspection. She had to use a spare bus.

"The mechanic tied a wooden block to the paddle, so it's all

PASSING THROUGH PROVIDENCE

set," Kenny said.

"Do you know where it is?" she asked him.

"It's in the first row."

She went outside and found it there. She started it, checking everything. The floor of the bus was dirty with papers and sunflower seeds. She hated kids who ate sunflower seeds. She picked up most of the papers with her hands because there was no broom. The dashboard had a layer of thick dust, which she wiped up with some napkins from the floor.

It was a nice day with the sun shining bright and warm. She opened a couple of windows to get some fresh air. When the bus was clean enough, she drove it around to get a monitor. A black man came on the bus wearing a neon yellow vest.

"I'm Jesse, how you doing?" he said.

She didn't say anything, driving the bus up to Union Avenue.

"How long have you been a driver?" he asked her.

"A few years," she answered.

"What's your name?"

"Eva."

"That's a nice name. Do you like to party?" He smiled at her.

"No, I'm married."

"Oh, I see." He didn't say anything else.

They came to the elementary school. She stopped the bus and the kids came on as noisy as ever, screaming and kicking.

"All right, let's quiet down!" Jesse the monitor made himself noticed.

Eva drove and made several stops, letting the kids off. Within a half hour, the bus was almost empty. One of the boys left was causing trouble in the back row. Jesse moved to the rear of the bus and yelled at him, told him to keep his mouth shut. The boy didn't like being told what to do, so when Jesse turned his back and was moving up front, the kid threw an empty soda bottle, hitting him in the shoulder.

"Did you see what he did? He threw a soda bottle and hit me in the back," he told Eva.

"I'll tell his mother," she said. "We're almost to his house."

They were there in a few minutes. His mother happened to be sitting on the front porch. The boy ran off the bus and told his mother something. The mother came down to the sidewalk and asked to see the monitor. Jesse came out and she told him not to yell at her kid.

"He hit me with a soda bottle," Jesse said.

"I don't care!" she screamed. "You don't yell at my kid!"

50
Bad News

Rossi drove to Saint Ann's Cemetery in Cranston. He tried every year to visit his father's grave. Sometimes he became too emotional and turned back home.

It was hard driving through the grounds to visit the dead. His father's grave was difficult to find at times, as if it moved. He stopped the car, then walked through the rows of stone before he found it. It was hidden by long weeds growing near the site. He pulled them with his hands and threw them aside.

Tears came to his eyes. He had memories of both good and bad of his youth. His father liked to drink and gamble, and there never was enough money in the house. Once his stepmother had to go on welfare so that they had enough to eat. When his father remained sober and worked, he remembered some good times, but not many.

He stood there a few minutes and said some prayers. Wiping back tears on his face, he had to go. It was just too much for him.

He drove to a garage near Olneyville. For the past few days, he was having trouble with the car. The starter didn't work sometimes and he had to hit it with a hammer. After a couple of blows, it turned over. He had been to the garage before and the mechanic knew him by name.

"What's wrong, Ross?"

"It's the starter, I need a new one."

"We only use rebuilts."

"Whatever works," Rossi said.

"I'm busy, you'll have to leave the car."

"No problem."

"Call me later."

He didn't live that far, so he didn't mind walking. It was good exercise.

The next day, Laurie had a doctor's appointment for the baby. Rossi took them in his car; it was running good again. He waited outside for an hour. He was trying to read a novel, something he hadn't done in a long time.

Finally, she came from the office carrying the baby. Getting into the car, she looked worried.

"What's wrong?" he asked her.

"It's the baby, she needs an operation. They took X-rays and found a hole in her heart."

"But she seems all right," Rossi said.

The doctor said, "If she doesn't have the operation soon, she could get worse."

"She'll get worse? Like what can happen to her?"

"She could die."

"Then she needs the operation," he said.

"It could cost several thousand or more."

"Don't you have insurance from work?"

"Yes, but I'm sure they won't pay for everything." She started to cry.

"Don't worry," Rossi said, "if they don't pay for it. I'll take out a mortgage on the house."

PASSING THROUGH PROVIDENCE

The baby rested in Laurie's arms. Her little eyes were open and she was smiling.

"Hi Anna," Rossi said. "You're going to be all right."

"I hope so," Laurie said.

"She's worth a million bucks," Rossi said as he drove.

51
A Trip to Newport

The bus that Boris bought broke down. He had to have it repaired, so he hired a special tow truck to pull it. It was a huge truck that could tow a house if needed. They brought the bus to the garage of the tour company.

While it was being fixed, the tour boss let him use one of their buses. The man told him, if he liked it, he would sell it to him for a good price.

Boris checked it over, and everything seemed to be working good. He had the money and thought about buying it. He used it for a charter to Newport, taking a class of middle school kids for a boat ride. It didn't take long to get there. He parked the bus near the water on Goat Island. The air was so salty, he could taste it.

There was a nice view of the harbor with all kinds of boats. Noisy seagulls were everywhere, and a flock of them flew overhead. The kids seemed happy to be there; it was a wonderful experience for them. A teacher led them to the tour boat. Boris was invited to go with them.

There were two decks in use and the kids filled them both. A young man detached the ropes from the dock and the boat started moving into deeper water. Boris sat on the top deck where there were several benches. Everyone was taking in the sights. There were boats of all sizes, and large yachts and sailboats were among them.

PASSING THROUGH PROVIDENCE

Old buildings of Newport slipped away in the distance. The captain of the tour boat announced over the loudspeaker some of the sights as they moved along. Soon, they approached Fort Adams and he gave a brief history about the place.

They continued through the harbor. "A lot of famous people have yachts here," the captain said. "That's Merv Griffin's boat on your right. He's the guy who started the game show Wheel of Fortune."

On the way back, they went by the old Kennedy complex. The huge house stood on a hill as a reminder of things past, where the Kennedy Clan used to picnic and play touch football.

A larger boat sped by them, creating large waves in its wake and really rocking the tour boat. The kids started screaming like they were on a thrill ride, laughing and holding on to each other.

The trip lasted almost an hour. Some of the kids wished it would never end. Breathing in the salty air made them hungry. They had box lunches waiting for them on the bus; afterwards, some of them were still hungry, so they went to a snack bar nearby for soda and chips, before they boarded the bus for the ride home.

Boris was sleeping late that night when the phone rang. It was his sister in Russia. She had some sad news: his mother died.

52
A Restless Time

The baby's operation was scheduled for tomorrow. Laurie couldn't sleep that night—she was worried about Anna. She lay there in bed awake, her mind full of thoughts.

In the morning, she dragged herself out of bed and lit a cigarette, then started coughing.

"You're making yourself sick," Rossi said.

"I'm worried about Anna," she said.

"You have to stop smoking. It's not good for the baby," he said.

"I know."

"You should take vitamins, like I do."

"Vitamins don't do anything."

"Well, you should stop smoking."

They rode in a silent car. Rossi took the day off from work, driving them to the hospital. The baby was wrapped in a pink blanket resting on Laurie's lap.

When they arrived, the people working inside were very helpful. Laurie had to give some information about her medical insurance and sign some papers, then they had to wait. There were other people there hoping to see a doctor too. A short time later, a lady came and took the baby.

Rossi watched television for awhile, then leaned back in his seat and closed his eyes. He wasn't sleeping though; he was saying a silent prayer for the baby.

Laurie couldn't wait any longer. She had to have a cigarette, so she went to the ladies' room. Her mouth was dry and her hands were shaking. She knew she had to stop smoking; she just couldn't go on this way.

Another hour went by. They heard nothing about the baby. They tried to watch television, but it was meaningless.

"I hope she's all right," Laurie said.

"She'll be fine," he tried to reassure her.

"We've been waiting a long time," she said.

Rossi closed his eyes; this time he was trying to rest his mind.

"I'm going to the ladies' room again," she said, leaving.

While she was gone, Rossi went to inquire about the baby. He asked a person working there if they'd heard anything yet. The lady said if she found out anything, she'd let him know. He returned to his seat until Laurie came.

"I hope we hear something soon," she said.

"I just spoke to someone over there. They're going to check on her and let us know."

After awhile, they were given the good news: the operation went well and the baby was fine.

53
A Cold Chill

Eva completed her bus run and went home. Her kids were at school and she had to do the housework. While washing dishes in her kitchen sink, she turned on the hot water and there was none, only cold. She went down into the cellar to check the heater and found the floor wet. She went back upstairs and woke Luis out of bed.

"I have no hot water, I think the heater broke," she said.

He stood up, putting on his pants and shoes before going down in the cellar to look.

"We have to call a plumber, I don't know how to fix it," he said.

They searched the Yellow Pages and found one close to home, but he couldn't come right away.

"I'll be there tomorrow morning," he said.

"I'll be waiting," Luis said.

"So we have no hot water for baths," Eva said.

"We have to wait until tomorrow," Luis said.

"For now, I can heat a pan of water on the stove to do the dishes."

"Good enough," Luis said, going back to bed. "Why don't you join me?"

"In a minute," she said, filling a pan with water. Suddenly, she could feel a cold chill in the room. Standing there, she felt a hand on her shoulder. She turned around and no one was there.

"Are you coming?" Luis was waiting.

She went to him in the bedroom.

"I was standing in the kitchen and there was a cold chill."

"If you feel cold, then get in bed so I can warm you up," he said.

She took off her clothes and slid under the covers with him, making all his dreams come true.

54
Return to Russia

Boris was on a plane to Russia. Earlier, he had taken a flight from Green to New York where he had a long layover. His old passport was still good, so now he was in the air flying to Moscow.

After several hours, the plane landed safely. He picked up his luggage and rented a car. His family's house was in a small town about ten miles from the city. He knew the way as he drove. It didn't take him long to get there.

Everything was still the same—the streets, the houses, even the school where he learned to read and write. He found the bakery open and parked the car. He opened the door to the shop and went inside.

"Do you have any donuts?" he said, getting their attention. They knew English from school. They were expecting him, but they were still surprised to see him.

"It's Boris, you're here!" They were his two younger sisters, Olga and Katharina, and they greeted him with hugs and kisses.

They talked about his trip on the plane and how his mother died. Later, he took his luggage from the car and followed Olga to the family house in back. She led him inside to the bedroom where he dropped his bags.

"I'll make you a cup of tea, then you can rest," she said.

There were some family pictures on the wall of the living room.

PASSING THROUGH PROVIDENCE

Boris took a minute to look at them. One showed his mother and father when they first married. There were a few of him and his sisters. He had some tea and they talked some more. Olga had gained a lot of weight since he saw her last, but Katharina was still bony.

The funeral was the next day for his mother. Boris dressed in his black suit and wore his sunglasses. Olga said he looked like a KGB agent.

There were a lot of friends of his family seated in church. Boris didn't recognize any of them, except for his old girlfriend sitting in the row behind him. She smiled when he glanced at her pretty face. The sermon lasted almost an hour.

After the burial service in the cemetery, Boris drove his sisters home in the rental car.

They were crying most of the way. He turned on the radio, hoping to change their thoughts. It didn't take long before they were home.

There was a reception for friends and relatives. They gathered in the living room and had tea and cake. Everyone wanted to meet Boris and give their condolences. He was talking with his old girlfriend and couldn't believe that she'd never married. While with her, his sister Olga got his attention by waving her hand. She wanted him to follow her into another room, so he did and she whispered something to him.

"You know, she's a prostitute."

"Who, Natasha?"

"Yes, your old girlfriend."

"I don't believe it," he said.

"It's true," she said.

He left the room and avoided everyone by going outside into

the yard. He found himself walking down the road to the nearest bar, where he stopped to have a few drinks. He was feeling pretty good later, when he saw Natasha walk through the door. She looked beautiful as she came toward him.

"Are you following me?" he asked her.

"I didn't know you were here," she said.

"I needed to get out of the house."

"Because of me?"

"I don't want to talk about it."

"I see," she said, lighting a cigarette. "Can you buy me a drink?"

"Sure," he said, "for old times."

"For old times."

"You know, I'm married."

"I know, your sister told me."

The bartender poured him another drink.

"She wants one too," Boris told him.

"A vodka martini," she said. "So how's everything in America?"

"Good, I have my own business now."

"I'm happy for you."

"So, Natasha, how come you never married?"

"You know, I was getting married, but he changed his mind. After he left town, things got worse. I lost my job, and I didn't have any money, so I started drinking. I didn't know what to do."

The bartender came with her martini and she drank it right down.

"You know, I'm an American citizen now, but my heart will always be in Russia." He finished his drink.

"So how's your wife?"

"She's the best, she helps me with the business and she can cook."

After awhile, they had another round. He wasn't used to drinking a great deal, and it was affecting his speech. He kept slurring his words.

"I better go," he said. "I think I had too much to drink." He stood up for a moment.

"Come with me for a short time," she said, rubbing his thigh.

"Go with you," he said, following her. He could barely walk straight.

They went into the street and it was getting dark. Her place was five minutes away. It was small with two rooms.

"This is my apartment," she said.

"This is it," he said, falling down on the couch.

"I'll make some tea," she said, going into the next room.

He could hardly keep his eyes open. "I had too much to drink," he heard himself say, then he fell right to sleep.

The next morning, he walked back to his family home. Olga met him at the door.

"You didn't return last night," she said.

"I stayed at Natasha's place." He went to the kitchen.

"You stayed with her?"

"Yes, but nothing happened. We were talking and drinking and I fell asleep on the couch."

"Honest?"

"I said, nothing happened."

"All right, I believe you."

"Do we have any coffee in the house?" he asked her.

"Yes, we do. You want a cup?"

"Yes, I'd rather have coffee."

She heated a pan of water on the stove and opened a jar of coffee.

"Can I make you breakfast?"

"That would be nice, thank you."

They continued talking about the past while she cooked. He wanted to know where there was a flower shop, because he needed to visit his parents' grave site one more time. She served him an egg omelet and toast. He was hungry, so he didn't waste any time eating.

"This is the best omelet I ever had," he said.

"Good," she said. She was a few years younger than him and divorced.

"Boris, does your wife want kids?"

"Yes, but why do you ask me?"

"Because our mother wanted one of us to have a family. Do you want kids?"

"I don't know. Why didn't you have kids?"

"Because my husband didn't want a family, so when you get home, you better get busy, big brother."

"I'll think about it."

He stayed a few more days, then it was time to catch his flight at the airport. He placed his luggage in the rental car and hugged his sisters one last time, before he left.

Flying home, he thought he was going to die. The plane hit stormy weather and there was turbulence. He had his seatbelt on as the plane descended a few thousand feet. When calm was restored, he started some serious thinking about his life.

His wife was waiting for him at Green. He hugged her and she gave him a kiss.

PASSING THROUGH PROVIDENCE

"Do you still want to have kids?" he asked her.

"Yes, whenever you're ready."

"Then, we better get busy," he said.

"Really?"

"Yes, really."

She gave him another kiss.

55
The Hospital Bill

Laurie was wearing something new on her arm, a smoker's patch. She developed a bad cough and the doctor told her to try it, so she did, going cold turkey. It was hard at first—she chewed lots of gum and was eating more. She learned to cook some meals for Rossi and was getting good at it.

Now she was watching little Anna crawling across the floor. The baby was feeling better and was so energetic, moving her little arms and feet. Her operation was a success and the doctor assured her that she would grow up to be normal.

Rossi was outside painting the house. He had a week off for spring vacation. He filed for unemployment benefits and was going to collect.

His father was a good painter, and he learned how to use a brush from him. He pulled the extension ladder out through the cellar window and set it against the house. The sides of the house were white wooden shingles and some of them were peeling, so he had to sand the sides first with sandpaper.

After this, he brushed on a thin coat of white primer, flowing the paint over the bare spots. When he was young, paint used to be cheap, but now it cost a fortune.

Laurie came from around the house, pushing the baby in a stroller.

"How's it coming?" she asked him.

"At the rate I'm going, it's gonna take all week," he said.

"What color are you painting it?"

"Light yellow, how's that sound?"

"Sounds good, anything's better than white," she said. "I'm taking the baby for a walk."

A squirrel jumped in front of her and ran across the lawn. Tommy Boy ran after it.

"He'll never catch that critter," Rossi said.

"No way," Laurie said, pushing the stroller down the driveway onto the sidewalk. She liked walking on Mount Pleasant Avenue because there were lots of trees casting down long dark shadows. She never used to walk before; now with the baby, she was enjoying it. She chewed gum as she moved down the street.

After going several blocks, she returned and headed for the house.

"I'm going to be real hungry tonight," Rossi said, seeing them.

"I'll cook you up something good," she said, going inside.

She put the baby in a playpen and went to check the mail. The letters were on the floor in the hallway. One of them was from the hospital. She opened it and saw a bill for the baby's operation, payable next month. She couldn't believe the amount and called Rossi in the house.

"What's the matter?" He rushed through the door.

"I got this bill in the mail for Anna's operation."

He could tell she was upset as he read the letter. "Holy smokes, fifteen thousand dollars!"

56
A Scary Dream

Eva wanted Luis to build a swing set in the backyard for the kids. He had to use a rack on top of the car to bring the material home. He wasn't a handyman, but he was learning. He worked in the afternoon, digging holes and mixing cement. His son Miguel was there to help him. He put the bars up one day, and the seats with the chains the following day. He wasn't sure of what he was doing, but he knew it was worth the trouble when he saw his little girls swinging on them.

Eva came outside to check on them.

"Mommy, push me," said one of them.

"Did you thank your daddy?"

"Thank you, Daddy," they said.

After awhile, Luis took a shovel and dug up a patch of ground, crawling with red earthworms.

"What are you doing?" Eva asked him.

"I'm making a garden, I'm going to plant some tomatoes," he said.

"Oh, good, I like fresh tomatoes," Eva said.

The girls were watching too.

"Daddy, look at the worms," they both pointed.

"I see them," Luis said. "They're good for the garden."

"How come?"

"They're good for the ground, so the tomatoes can grow."
"Oh."

Eva was smiling. She still couldn't believe she owned her own property. It was like a dream come true.

It was getting late and the sun disappeared behind some clouds. Luis was tired, so he went in the house to rest. He lay on his bed, drinking a beer and looking at a *Playboy* magazine. Soon, he fell asleep and was dreaming of topless ladies. It wasn't long before something grabbed him by the neck. He woke up choking with his eyes wide open. He didn't see anyone. It felt real, like a rope was around his neck. He lay there for a minute glancing around the room. Maybe there's a ghost in the house, he was thinking. He'd never believed in ghosts. He knew he'd felt something around his neck and it was real.

On the first of the month, the elderly lady on the third floor came downstairs and paid the rent, but the single guy on the second floor gave them nothing. He told Luis that his car broke down and he was having it fixed.

"So when are you going to pay the rent?" Luis asked him.

"In about two weeks," he said.

"Okay, then I'll see you in two weeks." Luis closed the door and looked at his wife. "There's nothing we can do but wait," he said.

57
Too Much Gin

Rossi finished painting the house. "I'm a one man machine," he told Laurie. He had blisters on his hands and his legs ached from standing on the ladder, but he didn't care—his house was done.

His car was giving him trouble again. This time it was the water pump. He was thinking of buying a new car, but he changed his mind after getting the bill for Anna's operation.

He was going to work one day and saw the door open to Sadie Smith's apartment. He looked in and found her lying on the floor. She was still breathing. He tried to wake her by calling her name. Getting no response, he dialed 911.

The rescue crew came right away, for there was a fire station around the corner. They took her to Roger Williams Hospital. Rossi still had her son's number and called him.

"I found her on the floor, and they took her to the hospital," he said.

He had to do his bus runs through Providence, so he continued on to work. He signed up for extra charters and was averaging forty hours a week or more. It really made a difference in his paycheck.

One time he had to take a team of boys for a high school wrestling match. He took them in the afternoon and didn't know the location in Woonsocket, but the coach did.

PASSING THROUGH PROVIDENCE

The event took place in a large gym. The stands were full of people cheering for their team. Rossi liked to watch the matches; there were different kinds, from lightweight to heavyweight. It was fast action and some of the boys were really good.

Sporting events always brought back memories to him of when he was on the track team, crossing the finish line first. Once an athlete, always an athlete at heart. It was late at night when they finished and he drove them back to Providence.

Sadie Smith returned home from the hospital three days later. She had a bump on her head, but she was in good spirits.

"I must've drank too much gin and passed out," she told Rossi.

"You have to drink more tea," he said.

"Tea, yeah that's a good one," she laughed.

58
A Nice Easy Job

Jack was back on land. He was driving the school bus again. What else was he going to do, for he was too young to collect Social Security. Besides, it was a nice easy job with summer vacation and weeks off in February, April, and December, plus holidays.

He just had to pass a physical every year, drug tests, written exams, plus a dexterity test and attend mandatory safety meetings. It was just a routine he had to go through; he could get use to it.

He enjoyed the cruise with his wife. She won two thousand dollars playing bingo on the ship and booked another cruise.

Jack was driving a small bus and one of the young girls was crying on the way to school.

"What's wrong with her?" he asked the monitor.

"Her puppy died," she said.

"Oh." He didn't know what else to say and kept driving.

On his way home that morning, Jack was thinking about the girl on the bus. He parked his car at the pet store and went in to get something.

Later that day, he had the same school kids on the bus. He gave the young girl who lost her puppy a gift. It was in a small cage with a canopy. The girl peeked into the cage and saw a pet hamster wiggle its nose, then she smiled.

PASSING THROUGH PROVIDENCE

"Thank you," she said.

"You're welcome," Jack said. He knew he did the right thing.

"That was nice of you," the monitor said. "You must like driving a school bus."

"Well, it pays the bills," he said.

59
A House Blessing

The man on the second floor never paid the rent and was giving them trouble. One night he had a party with several people and loud music.

"He's keeping the kids awake," Eva said to her husband.

Luis went upstairs and told him to turn the music down, so the kids could sleep. The noise grew less for awhile, but it didn't go away and it was still annoying.

The next day Luis told him to move somewhere else. The man said he needed to get some money first.

A couple of weeks went by and he was still living there without paying the rent. Luis had to get a law official to serve eviction papers, informing him to move.

Several days later, there was a knock on the door. It was the city inspector. He told Eva that he had some code violations to check on the second floor. She went upstairs and opened the door. He walked through the apartment.

"The man who lived here did this damage," she said.

There were bare electric wires coming from the ceiling light, kitchen stove pipes were loose, the toilet was broken, and outside, the bolts on the fire escape were coming off. There were some big holes in the wall too.

PASSING THROUGH PROVIDENCE

The inspector made some notes on his clipboard, then he told Eva she had thirty days to fix everything.

"We had to serve papers to get the man to move, so he did this damage," she said.

"Well, that's a civil matter, you'll have to get a lawyer," he said.

Eva was getting mad. "You mean there's no law to put him in jail," she said.

"Like I said, it's a civil matter."

"But he didn't pay me the rent and damaged my property."

"I know," he said, "there's nothing I can do. You have thirty days to make repairs." Then he left.

Late one night, Eva and Luis were sleeping in bed when there was a noise. Luis woke up and saw his stack of *Playboy*'s on the floor. They must have fallen off the table, he thought, and went back to sleep. Minutes later, a big hardcover book landed on his head, jarring him awake. He peered into the darkness and saw nothing. He wasn't hurt, just upset. A row of books were kept on the headboard shelf. He wondered how one could fall.

Eva was awake now and asked him what was wrong. He explained to her what had happened, then they rolled over, hoping to get some sleep without any other occurrences.

In the morning they were sitting at the kitchen table having breakfast.

"I think there's something wrong with this house," Luis said.

"What do you mean?" Eva looked at him with doubt.

"I think we have ghosts," he said.

"I think so too," she said.

"When that book hit me in the head last night, it was no accident."

"And I felt the hand again on my shoulder," she said.

JOHN FULCO

"What can we do?"

"I'm going to the church and talk with a priest, maybe he can do something," she said.

A few days later, two priests dressed in black walked around the house blessing it, then they went inside saying prayers, dowsing holy water in the rooms. Before leaving, they hung sacred crosses on the walls. After this, nothing strange happened for the next month. Only time would tell.

60
A Big Surprise

Laurie was doing better. The smoking patch was helping and her willpower was getting stronger. She was keeping busy with the baby, constantly changing Anna's diapers and washing her.

She found a letter in the mail one day that was forwarded from her old address in Cranston. It was from an insurance company to her deceased husband. It was a bill, due next month. She didn't know he had life insurance. She wondered how much it was for.

There was a phone number, so she called. She gave the person on the line the policy number on the letter and her Social Security number, telling him her husband died in an accident. He told her she was the beneficiary and would have to send proof of death papers before they could send her a check.

"I forgot what the amount was for," she said.

He told her how much.

"Thank you," she said in disbelief.

A few weeks later, Rossi woke up in bed and Laurie served him coffee.

"I have to make the loan on the house today," he said.

"No you don't," she said.

"And how are we going to pay for the baby's operation?"

"I'm going to pay it," she said, smiling.

"How?" Rossi was confused.

"Alex had life insurance. I didn't know about it until I got a letter in the mail, then I found out that I'm the beneficiary."

"How much did you get?"

"Enough—"

"You can tell me."

"I got thousands."

"You're kidding me, right?"

"No I'm not. I got enough to pay for the baby's operation and something for you."

"Something for me?" He was going numb.

"Look out the window."

He stumbled from the bed and couldn't believe his eyes. In the driveway, he saw a shiny new car.

THE END